MERLIN TAKES A FAMILIAR

MERLIN'S MAGICAL MYSTERIES
BOOK 1

MOLLY FITZ

Editor: Jennifer Lopez, Mistress with the Red Pen
Cover: JoY Author Design Studio
Proofreader: Jasmine Jordan

PO Box 873543
Wasilla, AK 99687

ABOUT THIS BOOK

My name is Gracie Springs, and I am not a witch... but I'm pretty sure my cat is. I first started to get suspicious when he jumped just a little too high while chasing after a robin in our front yard. I knew for sure when he opened up his mouth and addressed me by name!

The first thing he told me? That he doesn't like the name I gave him—even though "Fluffy" fits him like a warm sweater at Christmas. Now we've compromised on "Merlin the Magical Fluff," which according to him references his long and proud lineage just fine.

After that small matter was settled, he informed me that I must uphold his secret or risk spending the rest of my life in some magical prison. I agreed, not knowing it would turn into a full-time job of covering his tracks and fibbing our way out of some pretty tight spots.

When my boss at the local coffee shop turns up dead as a dormouse, things go from challenging to practically impossible... especially since all my coworkers seem to think I'm to blame.

Here's hoping my witchy cat can charm our way out of this one, because right now it looks like I'm cursed if I do and charged with murder if I don't. Yikes!

1

My name is Gracie Springs, and I've always been a pretty normal girl. I work as a barista while working toward my master's degree in Sociology. I've finished all my coursework but still haven't landed upon the perfect thesis topic. And I can't earn my degree until I do.

Oops.

Meanwhile I live in a small suburban town in Southern Georgia called Elderberry Heights. And the name fits it to a *T*, because most of my neighbors are somewhere north of seventy years old. I'm living in my grandma Grace's house, which she left behind when she chose to move south to a trendy retirement community in the Florida Keys.

She gave me the home where she raised my father and all my uncles, saying it was my early inheritance and that I'd always been her favorite, anyway—and not just because we shared a name.

She left all her furniture and decor, which means my house has at least three dozen hand-crocheted doilies and the living room is made up of brown floral couches and honey oak side tables. I don't have the heart—or the money—to change anything.

Grandma Grace also left me this ragamuffin cat that turned up at her doorstep only days before she'd been scheduled to move out and me to move in. The vet says he's a Maine Coon. I say he's much larger than any cat should ever be, especially considering all that stripey fur that poofs out from his body and makes him look like a literal fluff ball.

I guess that's why I named him Fluffy.

Keeping a cat I hadn't wanted was a small price to pay for being handed a free house, and over time Fluffy has started to grow on me. He's not exactly the cuddly type. In fact, every time, I've tried to pick him up, he's gone for blood. And succeeded in getting it twice.

I don't try to pick him up anymore, but if I sit really still and pretend I'm not interested, sometimes he'll help himself to my lap. Once he even purred.

Fluffy does love food and often takes a bite of whatever I'm having for dinner. He also enjoys running up and down the hallways in the middle of the night like a creature possessed.

I hadn't meant for him to be an outdoor cat, but he's such a good escape artist that eventually I just installed a pet door so I wouldn't have to worry about it, anymore.

That brings me to this morning…

I was running late for work, thanks to having a particularly difficult time following a new makeup tutorial from my favorite beauty Tuber. In the end, I scrubbed off the whole thing and went with a smoky eye and nude lip. That'd teach me to try something new so close to the start of my shift.

Especially since my mean old boss would take any excuse to dock my pay. He's still bitter that a popular franchised cafe moved in a couple streets away and cut his profits considerably. But he's also stubborn and not quite ready to admit defeat, which is why he's kept the whole staff on while slashing our hours and looking for any excuse to pay us less.

Great guy, that boss of mine.

I hadn't seen Fluffy since breakfast and wanted

to make sure everything was okay with him before taking off for my shift.

"Fluffy! Fluffy! Here, kitty, kitty!" I called and clicked my tongue, but he didn't come running. He never comes running. It's always up to me to find him.

And so I looked under the bed, behind the couch, and out the front window.

Finally I spotted him with his butt in the air and face toward the ground in that classic pre-pounce pose. Across the way stood an unaware robin bathing in the stone birdbath Grandma left behind with whatever few drops hadn't yet been evaporated by the hot summer sun.

Wiggle, wiggle, went Fluffy's butt.

He leaped, but the robin saw him coming and flittered away.

Fluffy flittered after him.

Not just a normal cat leap, either. He looked like a tiny feline athlete about to slam dunk a basketball. Up and up he went after that frightened avian target. He must have gone at least six feet into the sky and was still climbing up, up, up.

That's when he turned his head my way and saw me watching. Those emerald eyes bored straight into mine, and for a moment he remained stuck mid-jump just hanging in the air.

Then he turned again, and the sudden movement broke the spell. Fluffy came crashing straight back to earth, then skittered out of sight, leaving me to wonder: *What in the heck just happened?*

I chalked the whole gravity-defying cat episode up to poor sleep and an overactive imagination, then hurried my way over to Harold's House of Coffee.

Despite ignoring both speed limits and stop signs, I wound up three minutes late for my shift. My boss, Harold himself, stood just inside the front door waiting for me.

He tapped his wrist even though he never wore a watch and shouted, "When will you learn? Three minutes means three dollars, and since this is your second offense this week, I'm doubling it."

I snorted and rushed past him to clock in.

"Gracie! Aren't you listening to me?" he demanded, trailing after me like a demented duckling.

"Yes, you're docking me six dollars for being

three minutes late, even though we have no customers and you only pay us minimum wage. And even that's because you're legally obligated. Pretty soon I'm going to be paying you for the pleasure of standing around with nothing to do while our customers hang out at Mermaid's Brew down the street. Does that sound about right?"

Harold's face turned bright red. "The insolence!" he screamed. "If it didn't cost so much to train someone new, you'd be out of a job. In fact you're lucky that I—"

He took a step back, shook his head, and tried again. "Listen here, Gracie. You're lucky that—"

His words stopped coming as he gasped and crumpled to the floor. From hotheaded to out cold in mere seconds.

"Harold, Harold!" I cried and fell to my knees to check if he was breathing.

He wasn't.

I grabbed his wrist and tried to find a pulse.

I couldn't.

Ruh-oh.

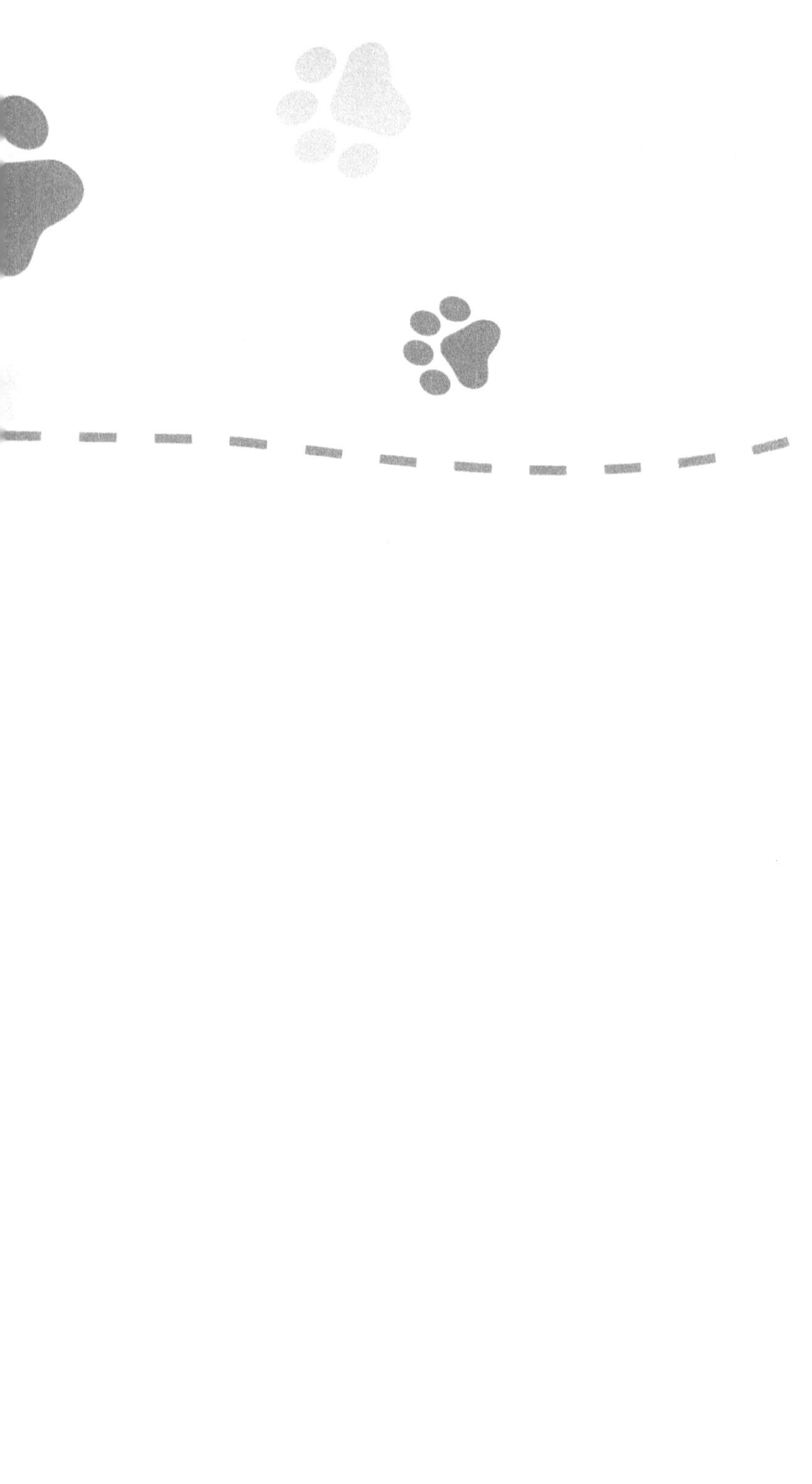

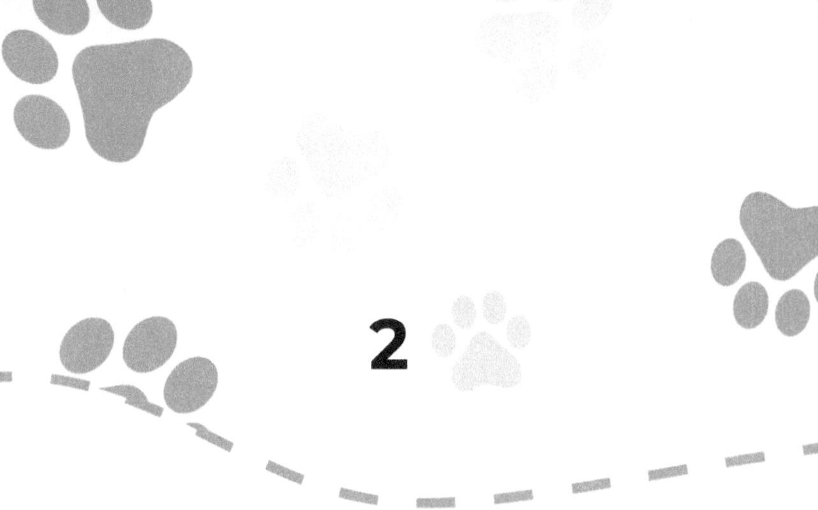

2

My boss had just dropped dead, right here in front of everyone—well, at least a couple coworkers and one customer who sat sipping a cold brew in the corner. Even though I couldn't find a pulse, I attempted chest compressions. But Harold was already gone.

"I'm calling an ambulance!" Kelley, our newest barista, shouted from behind the cash register.

Drake, our shift manager, tromped over to the door and flipped the open sign around, then drew the blinds.

"I'm sorry, Miss," I told our lone customer. "We're going to have to ask you to leave now. If you have your punch card handy, I can give you a couple extra points as an apology for the incon-venience."

Had Harold been alive, he would have fired me for that, given his propensity to nickel and dime both his staff and his customers for all they were worth. But I guess that didn't really matter now.

The woman took a long swig of her cold brew, her green eyes wide as she regarded me, then tossed the remainders in the trash can, gathered her belongings, and high-tailed it out of there. I couldn't say I blamed her.

Kelley rushed over to my side and glued herself there. "An ambulance is on the way."

"Won't do any good if the jerk is already dead," Drake said with a scowl.

"Don't talk like that," Kelley shrieked, clutching a hand to her chest. "A man just lost his life!"

"Probably a heart attack," I offered with a shrug. "It's sad, but it happens all the time. Harold wasn't exactly in the best of shape, besides."

"Yeah," Drake added with a sarcastic laugh as he crossed his arms and leaned back against the counter. "And considering his heart was at least three sizes too small, I'd say it had a pretty hard time keeping up."

I kept my lips pressed together in a tight line. Even though I agreed with Drake's assessment of the man, it was a terrible thing to witness his death. Add to that the uncertainty of my future employment, and today was just an all-around crummy day.

We had a few gawkers peek through the edge of the windows where the blinds were cut slightly too short and thus allowed a glance inside. One even knocked despite the CLOSED sign. Drake pounded on our side of the door and screamed threats at the would-be customers.

I decided to focus on my work even though there was no one to make coffee for. I cleaned down all the tables and counters, praying help would arrive soon. There was something so creepy about being locked in with a dead body.

I think Drake felt it, too, because he continued to pace and prowl, all the while muttering something under his breath.

By the time the emergency workers arrived, Kelley had taken up a spot on one of the squishy club chairs, her knees drawn into her chest as she sobbed silently.

Since neither of my coffee colleagues were in shape to play host, I welcomed the paramedics and the policewoman inside, then relocked the door behind them.

"He's right over here," I announced, walking them toward the back area that housed Harold's small office and gave the rest of us a place to stash our coats and scan our timecards.

Poor Harold lay on his back with his head slouched against the wall and his neck bent uncomfortably. One hand set atop his chest and the other lay splayed out at his side. His face had already started losing its color, giving him that waxen appearance that no amount of postmortem makeup could hide.

The paramedics bent to examine Harold while the policewoman remained standing at my side. "Is there a place we could go to have a chat?" she asked, her face giving nothing away.

"Sure." I led her to the one booth we had in the back corner of the cafe, a relic from the shop's previous life as an old pancake place. "Would you like a coffee or something?"

She shook her head and pointed to her shirt pocket. "I'm Officer Dash. And you are?"

"I'm Gracie. Gracie Springs."

She took out a notebook, licked her finger, and flipped to a fresh page, then drew a small pen out of the binding and held it poised above the paper. "And you worked for the deceased?"

"Yes. For the past few months."

Officer Dash scribbled away with a frown.

"Why is this important?" I asked, tapping my fingers against the tabletop.

"Just getting the facts down now in case we need to revisit them later."

"But what do you mean?"

She raised an eyebrow at me. "Ever heard the phrase presumed innocent until proven guilty?"

I nodded.

"Well, in this case, our stiff is presumed murdered until proven dead by natural causes. We can't just assume there's no foul play involved here, because by the time we get the coroner's report, we'll have already lost the opportunity to investigate the crime scene."

My head spun. There was no way Harold had been murdered. And yet...

"Wait," I mumbled, a horrifying thought settling into my brain. "You don't think I had something to do with this. Do you?"

Officer Dash smirked. "From what the dispatcher told us, you were having a heated exchange with the deceased right before he keeled over."

"Yes, but you couldn't possibly—"

"And were these fights a regular thing?"

"Yes, but I didn't—"

"Well, Gracie Springs. You better hope that Harold died of a heart attack or an aneurysm or some other kind of commonplace medical tragedy. Otherwise you are definitely at the very top of my suspect list."

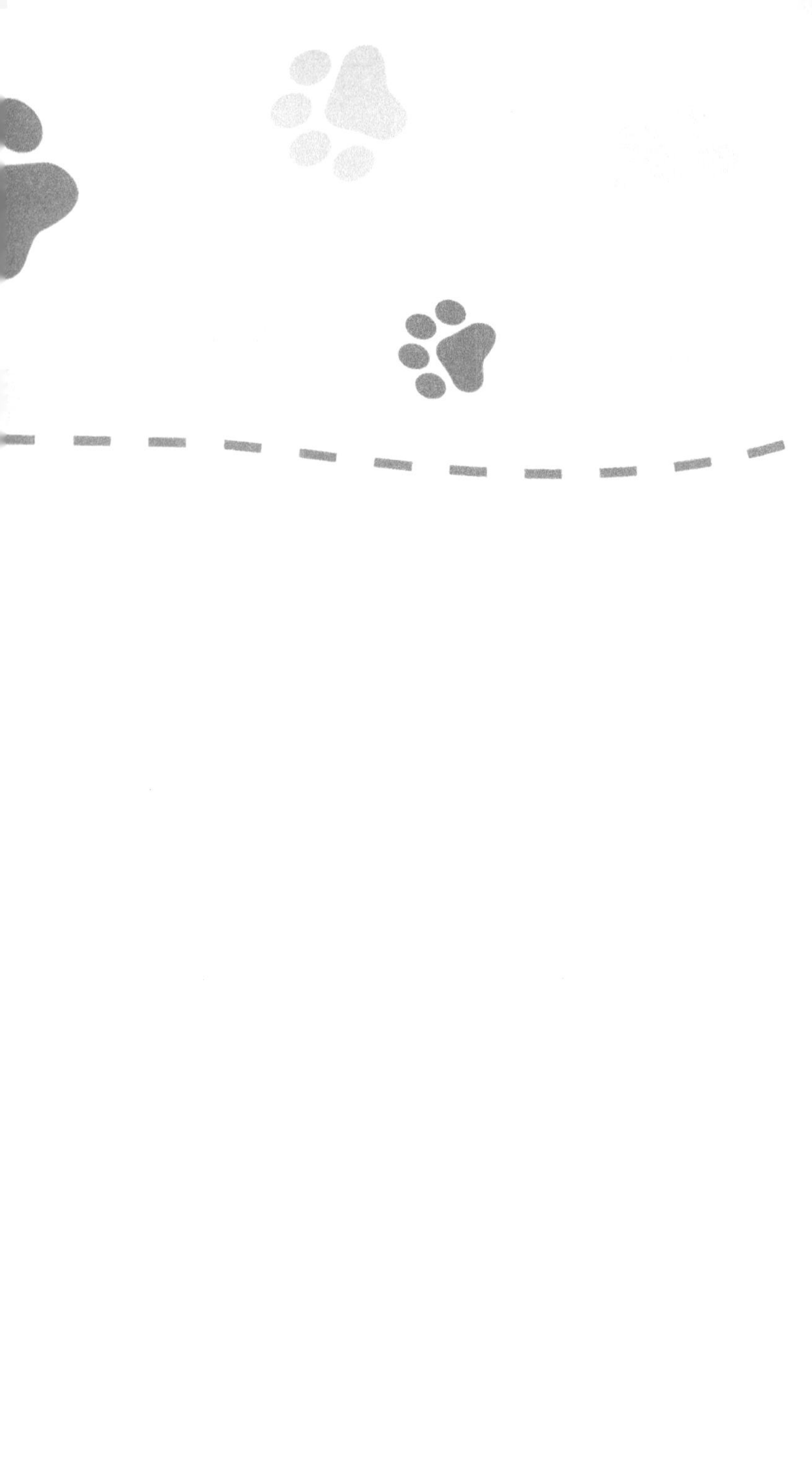

3

returned home physically exhausted and emotionally wrung out. Everything happened so fast after Harold collapsed. The severity of Officer Dash's implication didn't fully sink in until I finally escaped the coffeehouse and began my quiet drive home. Now that I had a moment to think, a few very important questions crowded into my mind. Why was she so sure that he had been murdered? And even more puzzling, why did she believe I'd done it?

True, lots of people disliked Harold, but nobody had a reason to kill him—least of all me. I mean, why would I when I could have just quit my job and never seen him another day in my life?

The whole thing made me sick... and terrified.

All I wanted to do was wake up from this horrible nightmare and go back to my normal, if a tad unexciting, life.

So I changed into my favorite matching flannel pajama set even though it was still the afternoon and the outside temperature was well over eighty degrees. Sometimes I missed my hometown in Northern Michigan where it was chilly more often than not, and my jammies—along with the added help of an overworked tabletop fan—helped allay the occasional bout of homesickness.

Right now, I wanted my mama. It didn't matter that I was an independent twenty-something. I'd been hurt, and I was scared. And just because I'd grown up didn't mean I couldn't turn to my mother in times of great need...

The fact that she didn't answer the phone when I called, however, meant precisely that. I hung up instead of leaving a voicemail, then fired off a quick text asking her to call me back whenever she got the chance.

Fluffy meowed and jumped up on the couch beside me. His whiskers twitched as he tried to discern whether I had anything worth eating. When he didn't find any food, he sunk his teeth into the edge of my sleeve and growled softly.

"Good idea," I said. "Today definitely calls for some ice cream."

I scooped up some of our favorite flavor—plain vanilla bean—into one of my lesser used breakfast bowls, grabbed a spoon and the remainder of the gallon, and settled myself back on the couch. The bowl was for Fluffy. I needed the entire container.

As we ate together, I began to share the events of my day with my feline companion. "That cop was so mean," I whined. "I mean, why would she just automatically assume I killed my boss? It was terrible. Just awful. To see the life leave his eyes. I don't think I'll ever forget it."

Fluffy sat up straight and cocked his head to the side. Sometimes, in moments like this, it felt like he could actually understand me.

"Mew?" my Maine Coon asked.

"Oh, yeah. I guess I should start at the beginning, huh? Well, my boss at the coffee shop, Harold. He died today."

"Harold is an awful name," Fluffy rasped.

"I know. I never thought anyone in the—" I stopped suddenly and closed my mouth up tight, then just stared at Fluffy for a long moment. Was I really so worked up that I was now hearing things?

I laughed at myself. "Silly me," I said with a

deep breath out. "Thinking you're talking to me, Fluffy."

"My name's not Fluffy," the cat said, then hopped off the coffee table and onto the sofa beside me. "So don't call me that anymore."

"Wh-wh-what?" I sputtered, rubbing my eyes until I saw stars. "I'm seeing things. This isn't real."

Fluffy clucked his little sandpaper tongue. "You meant to say you're hearing things, and no, you're not. I'm talking to you, Gracie."

I jumped off the couch and spun wildly around the living room. "Come out, come out wherever you are!" I shouted with a mad laugh, not really sure who I was confronting here. "The joke's up. Haha, you actually had me convinced Fluffy was talking. Yup, I'm crazy! You win! Now come out and fess up!"

Fluffy let out an enormous yawn, then settled down with his paws tucked into himself. "You are most definitely acting crazy. Also I already told you my name's not Fluffy, so will you please stop calling me that?"

I gasped, then sunk to the floor before I could pass out and crash down onto it. "This is not real. This is not real," I murmured, acting quite similarly to how Kelley had when she was balled up and rocking in that club chair back at the coffee shop.

"What's not real?" Fluffy asked, jumping off the sofa and striding over to me.

"You can't talk."

"I can talk, but it seems you're not very good at listening."

"Are you going to hurt me?"

"Of course I'm not going to hurt you. I need you to feed me, don't I? Silly human."

"What do you want from me?"

"The aforementioned food and also for you to stop calling me Fluffy. I much prefer the name given to me by my ancestors, thank you."

"Um... Okay. What should I call you?"

"The name's Merlin, and I come from a long and noble lineage of wizards dating all the way back to King Arthur."

"You're magic?" I asked with a quick breath in.

"Duh," my cat spat, and then I officially passed out.

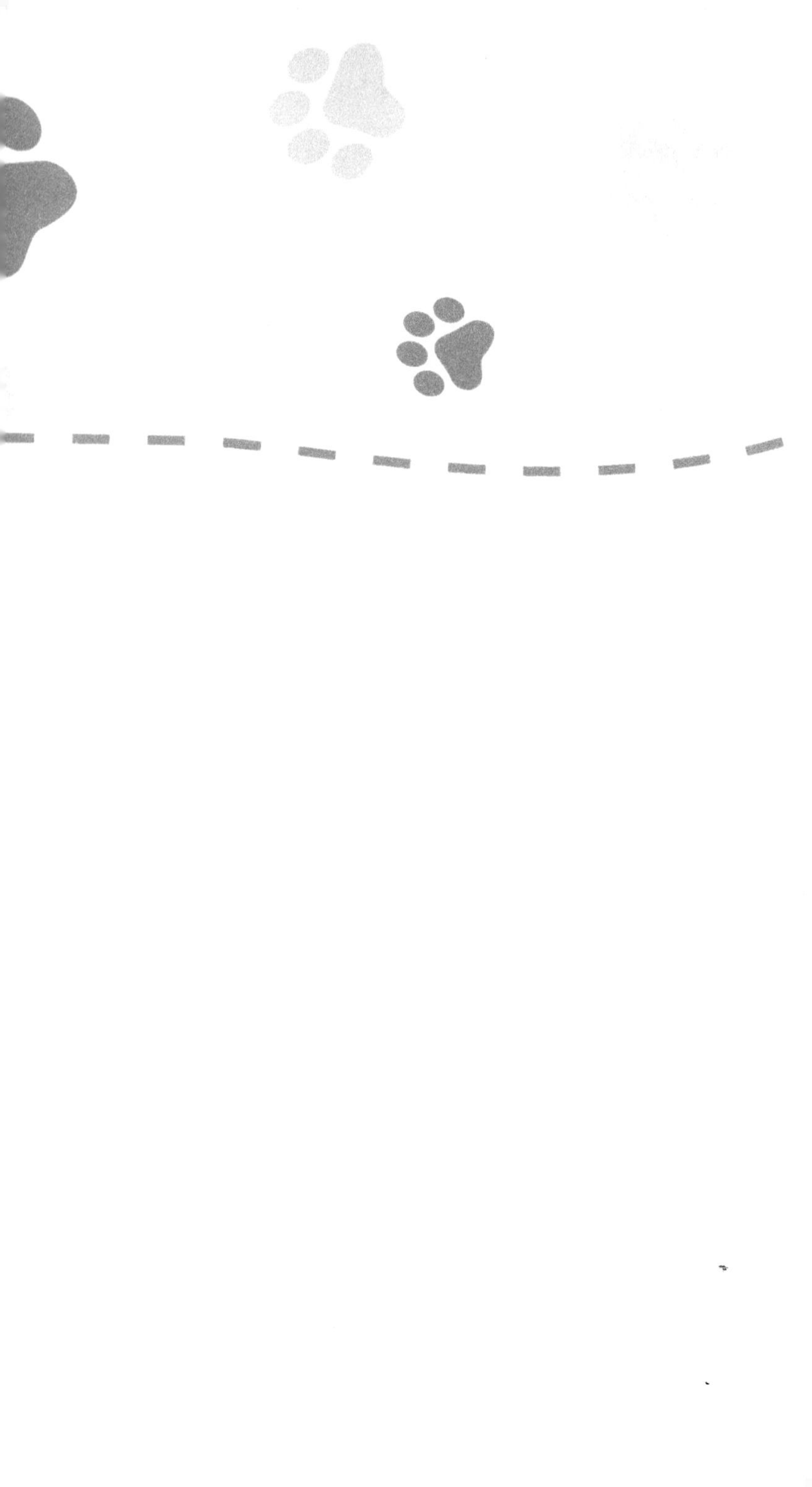

4

Night had already fallen by the time I regained consciousness. I'd like to say that I experienced a few blissful moments of ignorance as to the day's events, but that's not what happened.

First one eye squinted open... and I remembered my boss had died right in front of me and that I was a suspect in his possible murder.

And when my other eye popped open... I remembered my cat could talk and also claimed to have descended from wizards.

Ugh. I just wanted to go back to sleep and wake up when this was all over. Was it too late to drop out of school and move far, far away from this place?

Well, I was awake now, and I had to do something. I had no idea what to do about my cat, and I felt uneasy being home alone with him here in my dark house, so I decided to drive to the coffeehouse and see if I could find something that would prove my innocence.

Thankfully, I had a key from the many times I'd been forced to work both opening and closing shifts. I parked at the other end of the strip mall out of some small sense of self-preservation, then crept toward Harold's House of Coffee and let myself in.

A shiver wracked through me as I used my cell phone's flashlight to guide my steps toward the tiny back office. I probably shouldn't have been there, but I definitely shouldn't have been blamed for a crime I didn't commit. Maybe Harold's paperwork would reveal a secret mistress or embittered rival. I thumbed through stack after stack of timesheets, noting that despite having less seniority Kelley earned more per hour than I did.

And that jerk Harold had told me minimum wage was the best he could do! I continued flipping through the records of money in and money out, finding no alarming departures from the standard totals week after week. I was just about to move my attention away from the desk and toward the filing cabinet when a *clack-clacking* sounded just outside the office door.

I froze in place and willed my galloping heartbeat to settle.

"Please be a rat. Please be a rat," I whispered to myself when I realized it would be impossible to hide from an intruder, then grabbed the biggest, most solid object I could find—a stapler—and crept out of the office.

"You're about as stealthy as a one-winged bird," a deep, vaguely familiar voice said from the shadows.

And then Fluffy—I mean, Merlin—stepped forward, his pale green eyes giving off an eerie otherworldly glow.

"What are you doing here?" I whisper-yelled.

"I know you left the house to get away from me," he said, his tail swaying in a large sweeping motion behind him.

"What?" I said. "That's—no. No, I didn't. Um, how did you get here?"

He sighed, letting out the unpleasant scent of stale milk, thanks to the ice cream we'd shared earlier. "I used magic, obviously."

"Oh, um. Why? I can handle things on my own here?" I wasn't sure why that came out as a question. I guess my nerves were still rattled by the fact my boss was dead and my cat could talk.

"Sure, you can." Merlin scoffed at my alleged independence, then shook his head and continued. "Look, I don't care why you killed this Harold guy. That's your business, not mine. But the thing is since you're my familiar now, I'm going to have to ask you to stop taking wild risks with your safety."

"Come again now? I'm your what?"

"My familiar. All good witches and wizards have them, and you're looking at one of the best."

"I don't want to be your—"

"Too late! Since I confided my secret in you, we are now bonded. No take-backsies." That irksome feline had the audacity to smile as he announced this.

I swooned and staggered backward. "I'm sorry. This is all a little much. Also I didn't kill Harold."

"Sure, you didn't."

"I didn't! That's why I'm here. I'm looking for proof that someone else did it. Although the best option is still that he died of natural causes."

"He didn't," my cat informed me matter-of-factly as he sniffed at the air. "I can sense the rage and ill feelings in this place. It's thick like a smog."

I raised an eyebrow. "Oh, then you know who did it, too?"

"Not a clue, but it's probably better you let the police handle this. You'll have enough to keep you busy now that you need to learn the ropes of being someone's familiar."

"I really don't have the energy for this," I pouted, then let out a long yawn.

Merlin touched my foot with his paw, and a little jolt of energy ran through me—a sudden pick-me-up that was even more powerful than a double shot of espresso.

I stopped to gape at my feline companion. "Whoa, you really are magic. Aren't you?"

"Yes, clearly." He rolled his eyes at me, a gesture I didn't even know a cat could make. "Oh, and also, you can't tell anyone."

"I won't," I promised as my hands shook with fear. "Who would I tell?"

"Not my problem," he informed me, turning to trot away. "But if you do tell, you'll be immediately transported to the dirtiest, seediest, awfullest magical prison that ever existed."

"Oh." My hands shook even harder now, and I dropped the stapler. A loud clatter rang through the empty coffeehouse, and my heart practically stopped beating in my chest.

My cat returned with a sneer. "Stop futzing. You're my representative now, and I don't take kindly to being embarrassed."

Ugh. What had my life become?

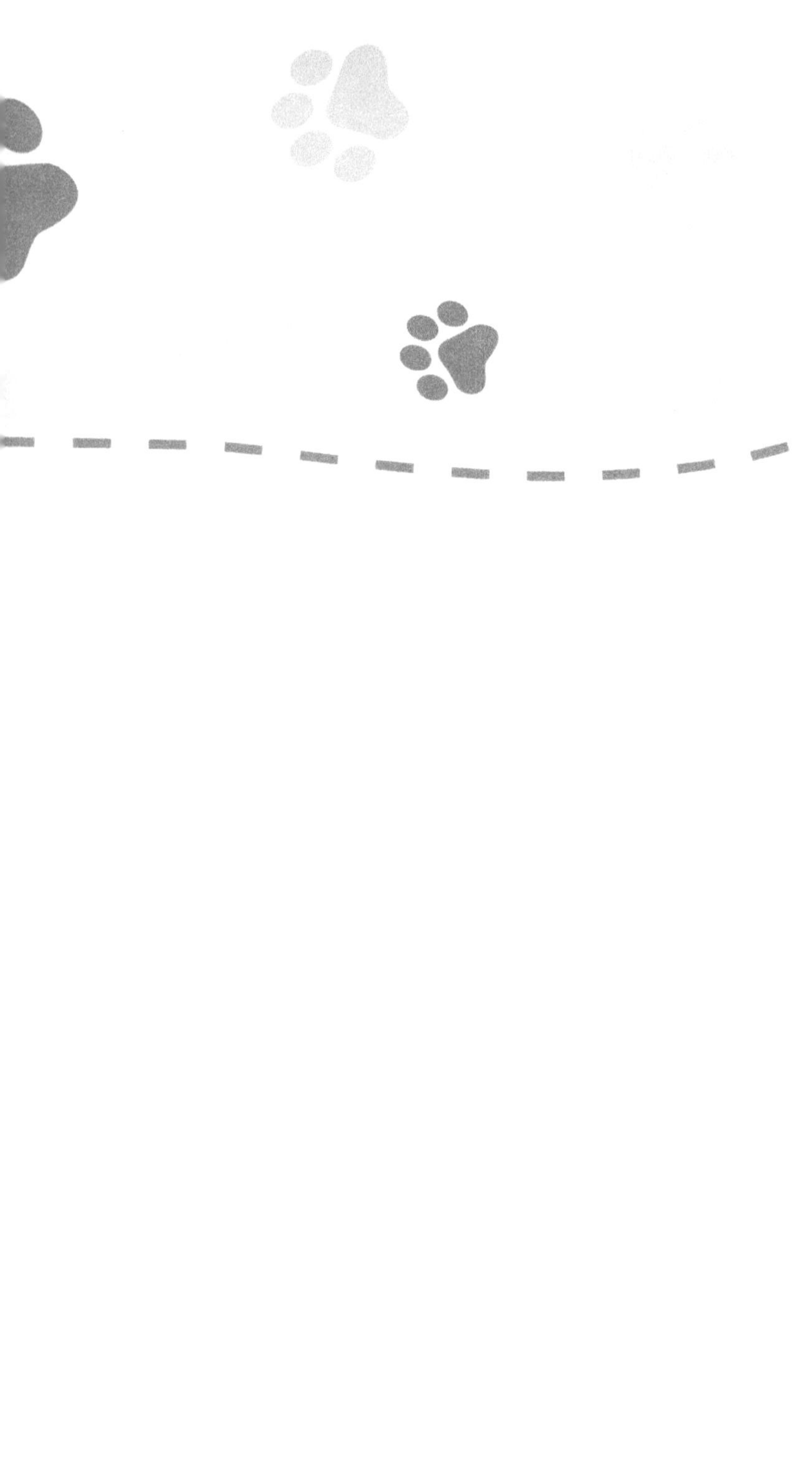

5

When we returned home, Merlin disappeared into the darkness, mumbling something about witchy business that needed seeing to and continuing my familiar education tomorrow.

I fell into bed in an exhausted heap and with a desperate prayer that tomorrow would be different.

I awoke the next morning to an insistent pounding on my front door. Upon squinting my eyes open, I realized that the sun already hung high in the sky. Normally my cat woke me in the pre-dawn hours to demand I refill his food bowl, but today he'd allowed me to sleep in. Why?

Knock, knock.

And who was that trying to break down my front door?

"I know you're in there," that unpleasant policewoman I'd met yesterday afternoon cried from the other side.

I groaned and pulled myself out of bed, quickly running my hands through my hair in a half-hearted attempt to tame it. When I flung the door open, Officer Dash snorted and pushed her way inside.

"Oh, please. Come right in," I muttered and closed the door behind her.

"Coffee?" I offered as I padded toward the kitchen and let out an enormous yawn so she could see firsthand how much she was inconveniencing me.

"Just waking up, I see," she noted with a disappointed shake of her head. "You sleep pretty easy for someone who just committed murder. Guess that makes you a psychopath."

I shook off her over-the-top insult and forced a smile. "Do you want the coffee or not?"

Officer Dash held up a hand. "None for me. Thanks."

I sighed and turned my back to her as I went about the business of rescuing my favorite mug from the dishwasher and sticking a pod in the Keurig so it could begin the brew cycle.

When I turned back around a couple minutes later with a full cup of coffee in my hands, I found she had made herself comfortable at my messy kitchen table.

I set my mug down and grabbed the scattered articles I'd printed for my thesis research, arranging them into a sloppy pile just out of the officer's reach.

She waited for me to sit and take a blessed sip before bombarding me with whatever news she'd come to share. "The M.E. has now confirmed that Mr. Harold Harris was murdered. We're still waiting on the full toxicology report to come back, of course, but you could save us all a lot of time if you just confess now."

I refused to be baited like this, no matter how insistently this detective clung to her false accusations. "I didn't kill my boss," I ground out from between clenched teeth.

"Uh-huh. That's what they all say."

"I don't know who 'they' are, but I'm telling you the truth about me."

Officer Dash widened her eyes and leaned

toward me in what appeared to be an intimidation tactic. "If you didn't kill him, then who did? Huh?"

"I have no idea. I'd only just arrived when he keeled over, so anyone could have come and gone by then without me knowing. Besides, I don't even know what killed him, so I can't really speculate." Okay, that was probably a bit insensitive, but this whole thing was causing me way too much stress, way too early in the day. I just wanted Officer Dash to accept my innocence and leave me be.

She grew even more frustrated, a sheen of sweat rising to her brow. "Are you even paying attention? Toxicology means poison. We're just waiting on the particulars."

"Poison, huh? Well, Harold pretty much always had a coffee in hand. We often joked that he'd set up shop primarily to save on his habit." I studied my coffee suspiciously, then deciding it was okay took another long swig. Heavens knew I would need all the caffeine I could get to make it through this conversation.

Officer Dash pulled a small notepad out of her pocket and clicked her pen. "We? Who's we?"

Shoot.

"Oh, um. Just the others who work there. Drake

and Kelley are the two who're usually around for my shifts, but there are others, too."

She studied me carefully. "So you believe one of your coworkers poisoned Mr. Harris?"

"I didn't say that. I honestly have no idea. I'm just as shocked by all this as you are."

"If the poison was delivered via his coffee, then you three baristas on shift had the greatest opportunity to pull off the crime," she pointed out with a shrug that came across as incredibly unnatural.

I shook my head. "I didn't say Kelley or Drake did it. Kelley was really, really upset."

"And Drake?"

Instead of answering, I took another long gulp of coffee. I didn't want to prove my innocence by throwing someone else under the bus, and there was no rule saying I needed to play Officer Dash's little game. When I lowered my cup, Officer Dash was still staring at me intently.

She stood and pushed her chair back in toward the table. "If I find out the poison was delivered via his coffee, you better believe I'll be right back here asking more questions."

"I didn't kill Harold, but I'll do what I can to help you find out who did," I called out half-heartedly.

She huffed. "They all say that, too," she said with a sarcastic smirk. "I'll tell your buddy Drake you said hi."

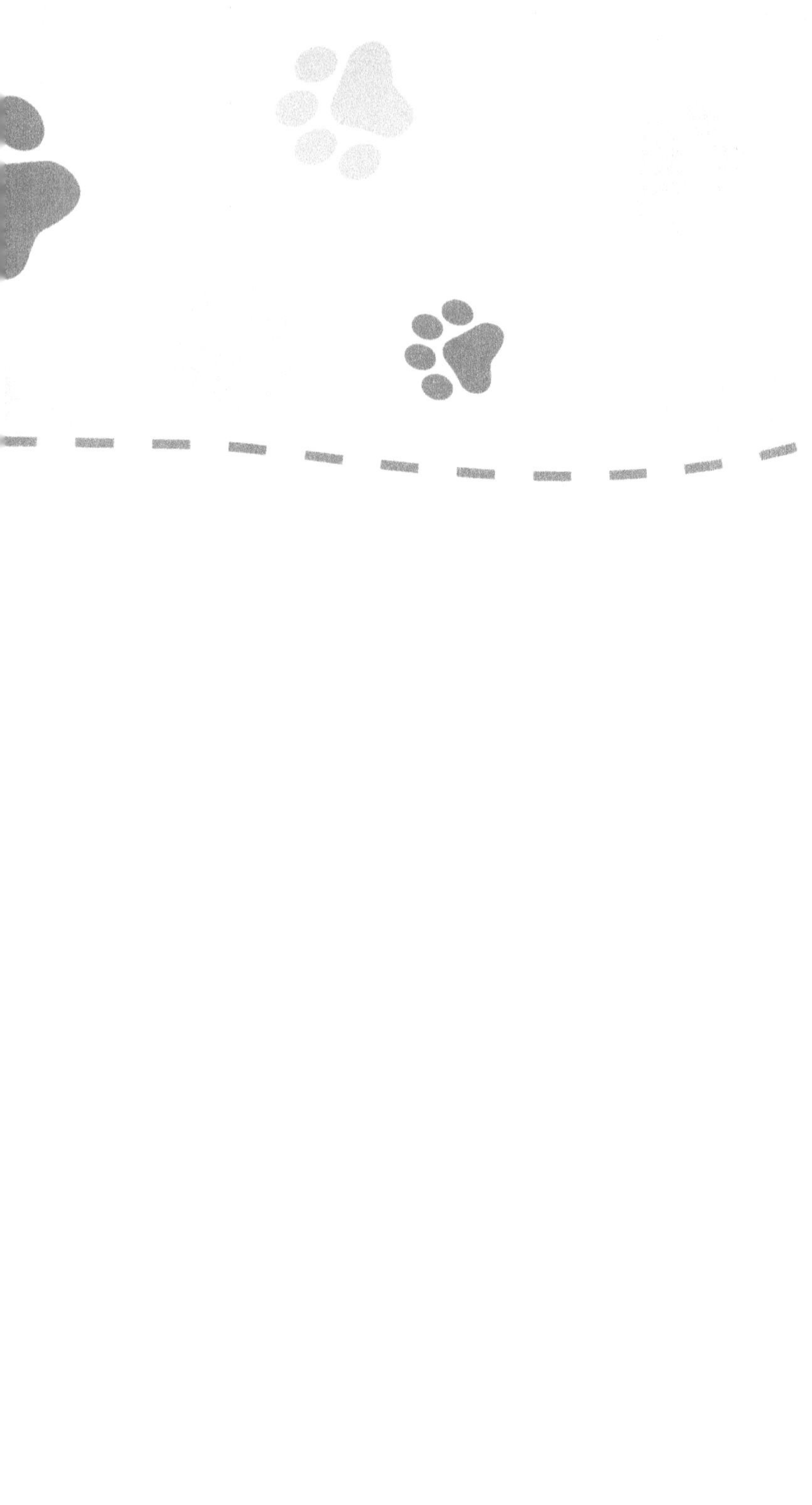

6

After Officer Dash saw herself out, I threw on a worn pair of jeans and a fresh t-shirt from my laundry basket, popped another pod into my coffee maker, and waited for it to brew. Before it even had a chance to finish, Merlin came racing in through the pet door, a cat possessed.

"Come, there's no time to waste!" he shouted, running laps around the kitchen with his tail flat.

"What's the matter?" I choked out. I may have started getting used to the idea that my cat could talk, but I was still having a hard time following his dramatics.

He stopped in place, fell over onto his side, and yowled. "Wrong! Now we're both dead."

"Dead? What?"

"A familiar should always be in tune with her witch. A quick response could very well be the difference between life and death, between freedom and capture," he lectured from his place on the floor.

I rubbed at my eyes. "You've gotta give me some time to catch up here. And to wake up a little."

Merlin hung his head and let out a dry laugh. "I chose poorly. Of course, I did."

"Insulting me isn't going to help me learn any faster," I pointed out as the last drips of coffee landed in my cup with a *plop* and a *plip*. "By the way, when do I get magic?"

Merlin's laugh came on loud and hysterical as he rolled from side to side on the linoleum kitchen floor. "Magic! You? Hoo, that's a good one. Thanks, I needed that laugh."

"It's not a joke. You forced me into whatever this is, the least you could do is make it worth my while."

"Oh, my dear sweet human…"

"Gracie," I reminded him. "I have a name, use it."

"Gracie," he spat out, then wrinkled his nose unkindly. "Would you be open to changing that?"

I scowled at Merlin as he dragged himself to his feet.

"Fine, Gracie, it is. And, no, you don't get magic. That's not a familiar's role."

He was proving to be even more tiresome than Officer Dash this morning. "Then what do you even need me for?"

"In addition to your previous duties of filling my food bowl and cleaning my kitty box, it is now up to you to be my face."

I stared at him deadpan.

"What part of that was a problem?" Merlin asked, tilting his head to the side.

I crossed my arms over my chest and sighed. "What do you mean by be *your face?* That makes zero sense. You already have a face."

"I can explain by sharing a story. Once there was this ugly guy with a long nose. He loved a gorgeous lady, but was worried she would reject him, so he struck a deal with a brainless pretty boy to—"

"Are you telling me the story of Cyrano de Berg-erac right now?"

"Oh, good, so you know it."

"And in this scenario, I'm your..." I raised my fingers in air quotes. "Brainless pretty boy."

"Sure. I mean you're a little better than brainless and a little worse than pretty, but it averages out."

"Sorry, I can't deal with this right now." I grabbed my fresh cup of coffee and marched toward my room, ready to slam the door in his face.

Merlin trailed behind me, too fast for me to shut out without spilling my precious coffee along the way. "I'm sorry. I forget how sensitive you humans are about things like that. I chose you because I believe you have what it takes."

"To be the brainless face of your operations?" I asked with a growl.

But Merlin either didn't pick up on my ire or chose to ignore it. "Exactly. I'm so glad you understand now."

"I'm sorry, but I have bigger plans for my life than that."

Merlin's eyes glistened with mischief. "What plans? Tell me, and I can make them happen."

I stared at him quizzically, afraid to ask for more.

"You don't have magic, but I do. Remember? Being a familiar is an important job, but not a thankless one. Many of the famous folks in your human history were secretly familiars."

I crossed my arms and glared at him. "Really? Like who?"

"Well, consider my namesake," he said with a smile stretched wide between his whiskers.

I balked at this. "Merlin. The wizard?"

"Ha, he wishes! The Merlin you humans know about was actually the familiar for an extremely powerful cat witch. His name was also Merlin, which makes it a bit confusing. The human Merlin wished to achieve power and fame in exchange for aiding his cat. But he became greedy and self-important, which is why the real Merlin cursed him to age backward. Meanwhile, he found a much more suitable familiar in a new human called Arthur. He only wanted power and prestige in the human world, which was much easier for my great ancestor to cope with."

"So Merlin was a fraud and King Arthur was just somebody's familiar?" I summed up.

"There's no *just* about it. Familiars are incredibly important. We witches do what we have to in order to keep you happy."

I raised an eyebrow in question.

"So could I be the next Lady Gaga?"

"That would take some talent. You may not have been born that way, but I can sure make it happen." Merlin paused and flexed his paws. "Is that what you want?"

"No, it was just a hypothetical," I rushed to explain.

"Careful then, because wishes that size only come around once. There's a lot of small stuff I can do on the regular, but truly life-changing alterations are a one-time deal."

"I'll keep that in mind," I promised, still not quite believing all this.

"As you should." Merlin appeared to be satisfied now. "Come. Let's begin."

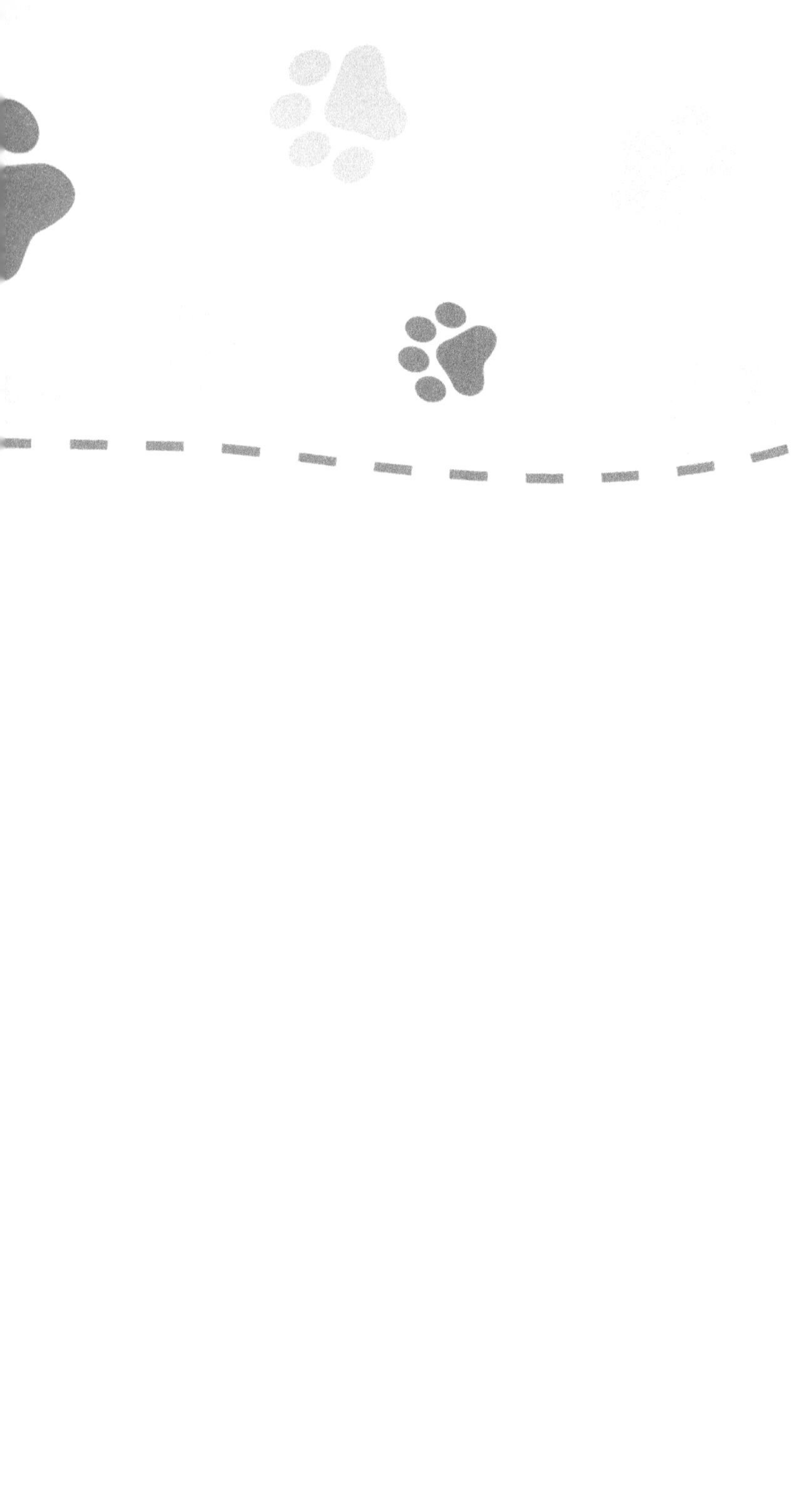

7

"Where are we going?" I asked as I chased my cat through the house.

Instead of answering, though, he ran through the pet flap and outside.

Hurriedly, I pushed my feet into a pair of cheap flip-flops I kept by the door, then swung the door open in just enough time to see him jump into the birdbath and splash around. I knew Maine Coons liked water, but it was still strange to see him enjoying himself in this way. Back where I came from, cats were cats—they hated water and they definitely did not talk.

"I saw you the other day," I said as I approached cautiously. "Yesterday," I amended.

Wow, that felt like a week ago at least.

Merlin stopped splashing and glanced over his shoulder at me. "Yes. And what did you see?"

"You f-fl-flew," I sputtered, wrapping my arms around myself in a hug. "After a bird you wanted to eat."

Merlin sighed. "First thing's first, I did not want to eat him. That guy owed me money."

I blinked hard. "Money?"

"Yes, money." He smiled now. "Secondly, I wanted you to see me. It was a test."

"Test?" A chill ran through me, even though the Georgia morning was already bright and warm.

Merlin rolled his eyes. "Stop repeating everything I say as a question." He stared me down, waiting for whatever it was he needed from me.

I gulped and nodded, still stuck on the fact my cat used money and that a neighborhood bird owed him some.

"I had to see how you reacted to your first glimpse of magic. Some humans can't quite handle it."

"And I did? Handled it, I mean?"

My cat looked me up and down then smirked. "You're still standing. That's a good start."

"What could have happened?" I demanded,

quite angry that he would knowingly put me in danger.

"You could have lost your mind," he said flatly. "Many do. That's why one must always exercise extreme caution when selecting and testing a familiar."

"So you mentally break people?" It took everything I had not to yell that. Still, we were outside in the middle of a neighborhood street. If someone happened by and saw me not only talking to—but arguing with—my cat, the crazy train would be at my door by noon, ready to lock me up and throw away the key.

My cat remained calm, casual, as if he were discussing meaningless trivia and not the very real facts of our lives. "Yes, not everyone can handle the existence of magic. A sad truth." Merlin straightened and puffed his fluffy chest out. "Anyway, glad you're still with me."

"Do I have a choice?"

He chuckled. "No."

"I didn't think so."

"Come closer," my cat urged, and I immediately did as told.

"What's this? What are were doing?" I asked, feeling awkward as we stood in the middle of my yard and continued to converse in broad daylight. Seriously, why couldn't we have done whatever this was inside?

"How to be a familiar, lesson one!" he declared with pride, then moved to the edge of the birdbath, balancing somewhat precariously. "Protect the cauldron at all costs."

"That's a birdbath," I pointed out.

He raised his arm high, then face-pawed. "It's a cauldron. The source of my power and my connection to the larger magical community. Without it, I am a witch at large. Not a proper witch at all."

I looked from the birdbath to him and back again.

Merlin sighed. "Lesson two, believe everything I say without question. For example, this is a cauldron. In the olden days, witches used giant black pots. But in the modern era, we use other commonplace items that are easy for a witch to access but go largely unnoticed by others. Observe."

He walked to the center of the small fountain and dipped his paw in. Instantly the thin layer of water began to glow a pale green, not unlike the color of Merlin's large eyes.

"Whoa," I said, the air whooshing right out of me in surprise.

Merlin tapped the water again, and it returned to its normal state. "This is why we cats choose to adopt humans. There is no guaranteed safe place on the streets. We need the guise of domesticity to protect our secrets. And also the shade of night. Naturally, we would prefer to keep away during the day, but it's easier to hide our true ways when most of you humans are tucked away in your beds."

I nodded along. Everything he was telling me made sense, now that I thought about it. Everything except...

"What do you need money for?" I asked, still stuck on his revelation about that poor robin who owed him money.

"You're still stuck on your own world. In mine, we... *MEOW!*"

"Huh?" I spun my head to see where he was looking and caught sight of a neighbor power-walking by.

She smiled and waved a hello, and I could swear I recognized her from somewhere. I just didn't know where.

But then just as quickly as she'd approached, she passed out of view.

I turned back to my cat, whose tail flicked

wildly as it hung down from the stone bath. "Watch out for that one," he growled.

"What? Why? She seemed friendly enough."

He sneered unkindly as he stared in the direction the woman had gone. "Remember lesson number two?"

"Trust everything you say?"

"Yes. That was Virginia. She's the familiar for a very troublesome witch who lives on the other side of town. Luna," he bit out.

"Did she come to spy on us?"

Merlin jumped down from the bath. "I wouldn't put it past her. Luckily, the cauldron is protected from other magical practitioners and their familiars. Come. Let's return inside where we cannot be watched by those who would do us harm."

Harm? It seemed I'd only survived the first of many trials when it came to joining my cat in his magical world, which left one question playing on loop in my mind: *WHY ME?*

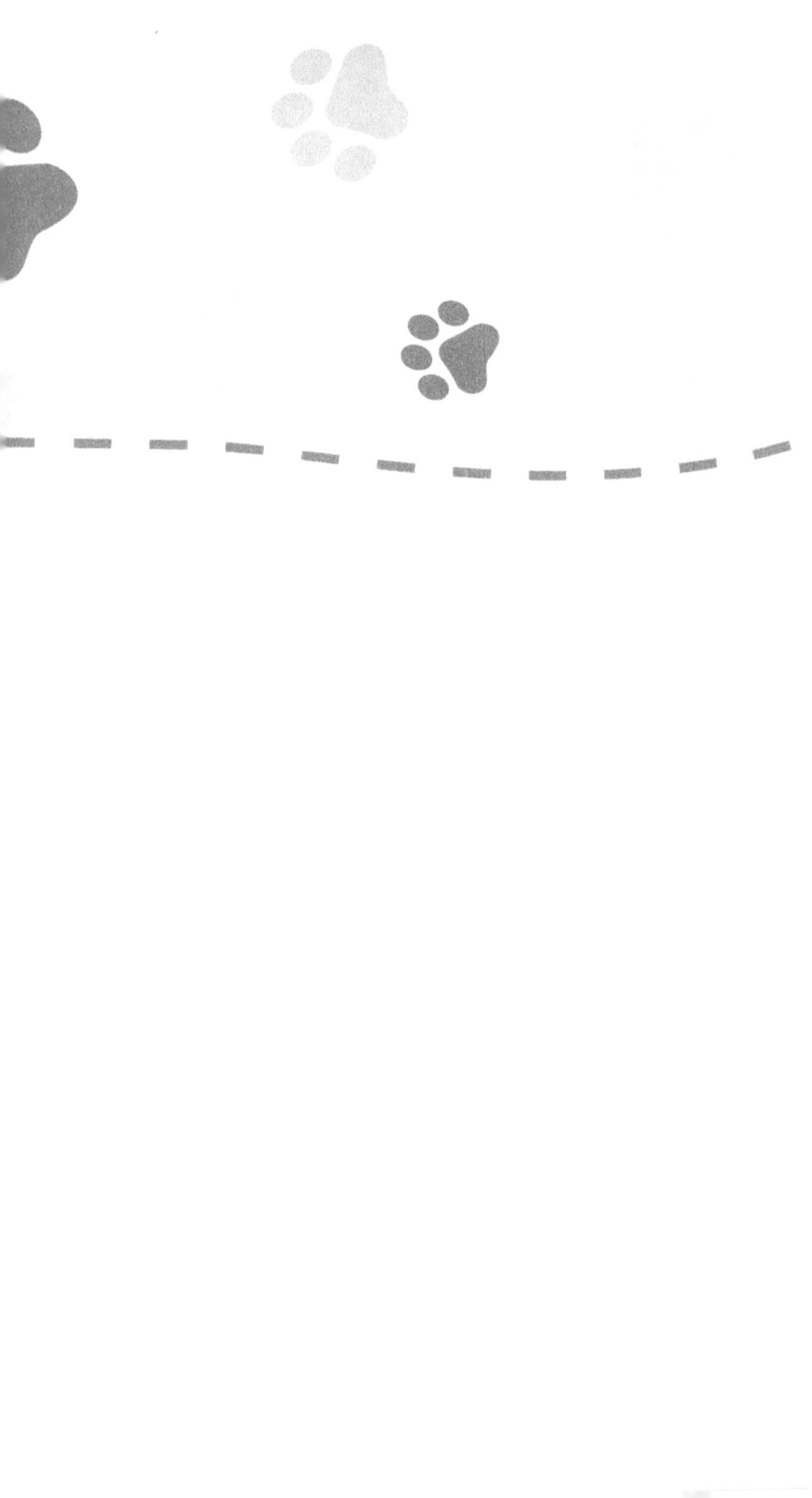

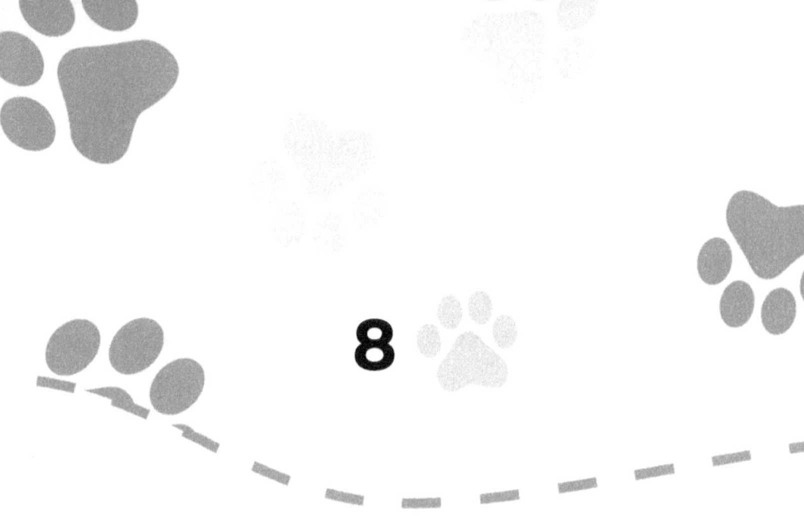

8

"We're going to Luna's," Merlin announced as soon as I'd shut the door firmly behind us. Of course, I didn't like this one bit.

"What? Why?" I moaned.

Unfortunately, Merlin remained steadfast in his demands. "If she's spying on us, that means she herself probably has something to hide."

"We're going to break and enter based on a probably? In case you haven't noticed, I'm already a suspect in a murder investigation!" I exploded, and I had to admit it felt good to yell after working so hard to keep it together outside.

"Lesson number two," he reminded me yet again, and I could already tell that this would be my least favorite of all the lessons, no matter what came next.

I huffed and crossed my arms. He couldn't make me do something I didn't want to do… Could he?

Merlin softened a bit. "Look, I know this is all new to you, but you have to trust me. I will protect you. And right now, protecting you means making sure Luna doesn't try something while I'm working to get my new familiar on board. We're both incredibly vulnerable right now, which means we must be vigilant."

He paused to suck in a deep breath here, then resumed in an even more somber tone. "You think human prison is scary? It doesn't hold a candle to the living horror that is a magical prison. If Luna exposes us, then we'll both go there with no hope of ever getting out. You get taken to human prison, I can break you out in a blink and help you create a new identity. Trust me, this Harold guy's murder is the least of our problems right now."

"Okay," I said, too tired to argue any longer and too afraid to learn any more about the possible repercussions of failing to do this familiar thing the right way.

He studied me with those curious green eyes of his and asked, "Okay what?"

"I trust you," I said, praying I wouldn't come to regret this assertion.

"Really? I expected you to put up more of a fight."

I shrugged. "What good would that do if we're just going to end up doing what you want, anyway?"

"I'm glad you agree." Merlin nodded, then blinked slowly two times.

I must have blinked, too, because one second we were standing at the edge of my kitchen, and the next I found myself under the shade of an unfamiliar magnolia tree by a small ranch-style home with a carefully tended garden.

I took a step back, pushing myself against the tree for support.

"What... What just happened?" I gasped.

Merlin stalked toward me and snickered. "Your first teleportation. So sweet."

"Teleportation?" I whisper-yelled, in case anyone was nearby and paying attention to us. "Next time give me a little notice, please."

"No," he said firmly. "It's much easier if you don't know it's coming."

I groaned and clutched at my head. Really that was just for show, though, because other than being shocked witless, I felt perfectly fine. "Where are we?"

"Luna's. Now c'mon." Merlin turned away from me and began trotting toward the back of the nearby house, his fluffy striped tail held high and proud.

"Wait. How are we going to get in?" I called after him.

But Merlin just ran faster, then jumped into a window box fitted with perky yellow daffodils.

I crept after him, one second moving through soft, spongy grass and the next stomping across a smooth hardwood floor. Great, now we were inside the house.

"Stop doing that," I hissed.

"Stop complaining," he hissed back, "and help me look."

"For what?" I said, taking in the homey decor.

Luna's owner—or familiar, I guess—certainly loved floral prints. They covered everything. I was pretty sure I'd seen that exact couch pattern on a pregnant B-list celebrity once upon a time. In addition to the floral fabric, drapes, and decor, more than a dozen vases of fresh-cut flowers filled the modest home.

I couldn't help but sneeze in response.

"Luna's a garden witch," Merlin explained when he caught me staring.

"What kind of witch are you?" I asked, mouth agape. First I learn that witches are real, then I find out they come in multiple flavors.

"Sky," he informed me placidly.

But my head was positively spinning from all the new information flying at me in rapid succession. "Come again now?" I squeaked. This seemed like one thing I just couldn't let go without getting at least some kind of quick explanation.

"I'm pretty well-rounded, but my specialty pertains to things that come from the sky. You know, wind, water, ice. The occasional burst of electricity, if the mood is right."

Finally, part of this was beginning to make some sense. "Oh, so you're all elemental? Like Pokémon."

His expression instantly turned dour. "No, not like a children's video game."

"Yeah, actually, I think it is. Luna's a garden witch, so plants and earth, right? That would make her grass and ground type," I recited, glad the many hours I'd invested playing Pokémon Go were good for more than just getting my steps in. "And you're water, flying, and ice, so you're kind of an even match. I suggest you use your ice powers in battle."

"This is not a game, and there are no battles. Now stop yammering and help me search for anything suspicious."

"Like that?" I asked, pointing to an old leather journal that lay open on the coffee table.

"No," Merlin began, but then he turned to look where I was pointing, and his eyes lit with delight. "Actually, yes. Good job. Now grab the book, and let's get out of here before someone notices our intrusion."

Well, he certainly didn't have to tell me twice. I hustled for that journal as fast as my flip-flopped feet would carry me, more than ready to head home.

9

Merlin blinked once, and I braced myself for another unnerving journey by teleportation. Before he could blink a second time, however, a nearby flower vase shattered and the thorny stems flew to my cat, locking him in place.

"Well, well, well..." A husky female voice floated toward us from the doorway. I hadn't even heard anyone enter. How could we have been so careless?

I craned my neck, too afraid to move the rest of me, and spotted a lanky white cat with bright green eyes staring right back at me.

"Luna," Merlin growled. "What do you want?"

She stalked over to him and slowly circled her

entrapped rival. "I think I should be the one asking questions here, since you're the one who broke into my house."

"I owe you nothing," Merlin spat and hissed.

While the two felines continued to argue, I carefully slipped the journal we'd found into the waistband of my pants.

"Why was your familiar at my house?" Merlin demanded. He looked so pathetic in that cage of flower petals and stems.

"Why is your familiar *in* my house? We can do this all day, Fluffy." She cackled at him, leaving no doubt who was the wicked witch in this scenario.

"His name's Merlin," I corrected angrily and grabbed for the white cat. Even though I didn't have magic, I did have almost one-hundred and fifty pounds on the skinny feline. Surely, I could overpower her.

But no. She escaped my reaching arms and turned back to hiss at me. "I'll only tell you this once, so make sure you're paying attention." Luna's back arched and her tail grew extra poofy. "If you ever break into my house again, I won't be so forgiving a second time."

I gulped hard, choosing not to point out that we teleported in, that there was no breaking at all.

Luna inched forward with claws extended. "What are you, stupid? Get out of here!"

I didn't need to be told twice. I picked up Merlin, thorny cage and all, and bolted through the front door. Outside now, I ran toward the street, which I could just barely see in the distance. Luna's large front yard sat at the intersection of two side streets. I tried to read the signs as I got closer but struggled to make out either very clearly.

Persimmon, I read just as my feet made contact with the pavement. Now that we'd stepped off Luna's property, the thorns and flowers that held Merlin fell away.

He jumped from my arms, shook off, blinked once, twice... And we were back home.

"All that for nothing," he mewled, padding toward his water bowl then taking a few long laps to refresh himself.

"Not for nothing," I revealed, tugging the filched journal from my waistband and bringing it into view.

"Gracie," my cat exclaimed. "Good girl. Very good girl."

I basked in his praise despite his dehumanizing tone. "I can see why you don't much care for Luna," I added softly. "Or the name Fluffy. I'm sorry."

"She'd have killed me if you weren't there," he said with a casual shrug. "She's been like that ever since I dumped her to take my place as a full witch."

I threw my hands up and took a step back. "Whoa, whoa, whoa. Back up there."

Merlin turned away but kept one eye trained on me from the side. "A cat doesn't become a full witch until he takes a familiar."

"Not that part. The dumping part?" I clarified, wondering why he hadn't told me this bit of his history with Luna in advance of our trespassing—and me stealing the journal.

Merlin yawned and stretched his back legs lazily. "Oh, yeah. We used to date. Not a big deal."

"Actually, it seems like a very big deal," I corrected, hoping he would tell me more.

"It's not my fault the rules state that no two witches may live under the same roof. It was fine when I was stray, but things change. There was no way I'd give up my awesome powers in favor of a fling. Nope. Anyway... No need to dredge up the past when we have our futures to worry about. Now show me the book," Merlin commanded without a second thought about his past love affair.

I tromped over to the couch and set the journal

in my lap so we could read through it together. "What is all this?" I asked, squinting at the strange series of symbols interspersed with sketches of various flora and fauna.

"It appears to be a grimoire. Not her primary one, mind you, but something new she's working on."

"A spell book? Do you have one of those, too?"

He nodded, continuing to study the page. "I have many, but I would never leave them in plain sight."

"Where are they?" I wondered aloud.

"That's privileged information, aka on a need-to-know basis. And you don't need to know right now."

"Ouch. Okay."

Merlin mumbled to himself as he flipped through the pages, completely unbothered by the fact that he'd hurt my feelings.

"So what are we looking at here?" I asked after a little while of watching, waiting, and understanding absolutely nothing.

"She's developing a new potion. A powerful one. But she doesn't seem to quite have it yet."

I stared at the book harder but still couldn't make heads or tails of it. "To do what?"

"I can't quite tell. This is all garden witch stuff. They're big on brews. Me? Not so much."

"Do you think it could be a poison?" I asked, thinking of poor Harold. Yeah, he may have been stingy and mean, but he certainly didn't deserve to be murdered over it.

Merlin immediately picked up my suggestion and ran with it. "You think Luna could be behind Harold's death?"

I nodded. "Yeah. I mean, why not? We don't really have any other suspects that make sense."

Merlin slammed the journal closed. "A very interesting theory. She may have been trying to get to you, but nabbed Harold instead."

I gasped, unaware of just how much danger I'd been in this whole time, how much danger I was still in. "She would do that? Kill me?"

"Duh." Merlin yawned as if this very important conversation bored him. "Luna is very dangerous, and she has it out for me, which means now she has it out for you, too."

"Maybe you shouldn't have broken her heart then," I mumbled, adding to the long list of reasons why I was very upset with my cat that day.

If only I'd have adopted a dog instead…

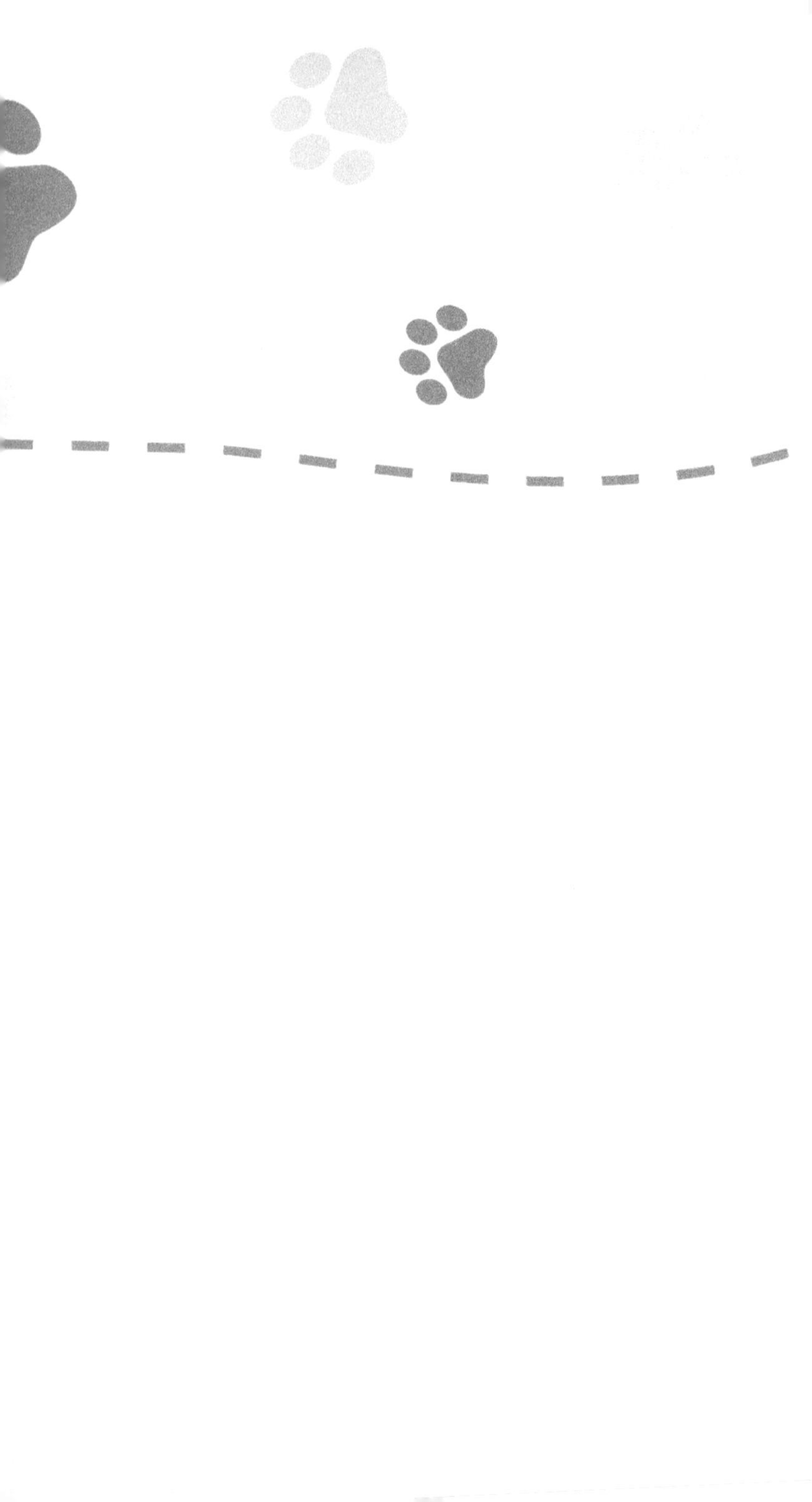

10

"I have to get to work," I said before shuffling my way toward the shower. We'd spent the better part of the last hour poring over that stolen grimoire and still had nothing to show for it. Well, except for my poor frazzled nerves.

"If Luna's so dangerous, perhaps you should return that journal," I shouted back toward Merlin before I closed the door and enjoyed some much-needed time to myself.

And he seemed to have taken my advice, because by the time I finished getting ready for my shift, neither he nor the journal were anywhere to be seen.

Honestly, I didn't know whether I was expected to show up for work that day, given the whole crime scene thing, but I decided it would be best to at least try to honor my responsibilities to the late Harold.

When I reached the coffeehouse, I found that it was still blocked off by police tape but that my coworker Kelley was moving about inside.

I let myself in, too.

Kelley glanced up suddenly from her place behind the glass pastry display case. "Oh, hi, Gracie," she said with a frown.

"How are you holding up?" I asked gently, coming over to stand beside her.

She shrugged. "Honestly, I don't know."

I glanced down at her hands, but they were empty. In fact, Kelley appeared to be doing nothing more than standing there in a mournful trance.

She'd been upset while we were waiting for the police yesterday, but I'd assumed that was more of an in-the-moment reaction. If possible, she seemed even more torn up today.

And that made me feel guilty that I hadn't spent any time mourning for Harold. Instead I was too focused on my worry that I might be pegged with his murder.

Even if Harold had been a bad boss, I still wanted to be a good person. Maybe if I helped

Kelley now, it would make up for my earlier failures.

"Yeah, it's hard," I said, keeping my eyes downcast. "He may not have been the best boss, but he was still a person we knew."

Kelley sobbed into her hands. "Not me. I hardly knew him. Not yet. I thought we'd have more time."

I didn't know Kelley all that well myself. I hadn't realized she'd wanted more than a casual work acquaintanceship. Had she been crying out for a friend, and we'd all been too busy to catch on? If so, I felt horrible about it.

Kelley had only been working at our coffee shop for about a month. She was a sweet girl who'd recently graduated high school and moved to our area for a gap year. I always wondered why she'd chosen to move to rural Georgia rather than backpack through Europe, but who was I to judge? Maybe she'd inherited a house just like I did. I could have asked, though. I should have asked.

I placed a hesitant hand on her shoulder. "Trust me," I said with a small smile. "You aren't missing much."

She turned to me with red-rimmed eyes. "Aren't I, though? I've spent my whole life wondering about him, imagining how it would be when I finally got to meet him face to face, but now we'll never get the chance to form a real relationship."

The revelation slammed down on me like a falling stack of bricks. "Kelley, was Harold...?"

"My dad," she finished, reaching into her pocket and pulling out a crumpled tissue. "He dated my mom way back when. By the time she found out she was pregnant with me, they'd already broken up and he'd moved away."

I hugged her hard. "I'm so, so sorry."

She tried to smile, failed. "I guess I wasn't meant to have a dad. I also guess there's no reason for me to stick around here anymore. I never should have come. That police officer says my dad was murdered. What if it was my fault somehow?"

"Oh no, sweetie. It definitely wasn't your fault," I assured her, but Kelley was not easily assured.

"Think about it," she said, knitting her brows together in frustration. "I show up in town, and a month later he's dead. That can't be a coincidence."

"Of course it's a coincidence. A horrible one, but definitely not your fault. You aren't responsible for your parents' decisions, and you're definitely not responsible for Harold's death."

She blinked up at me. "Do you mean it?"

I bobbed my head vigorously. "Yes, absolutely."

Finally Kelley chanced a small smile. "Thanks."

"If you've got some time, I can tell you some stories about him."

Her smile grew wide and bright. "Really?"

"Yeah. It's not like we're open for business. Let's grab ourselves a snack and settle in for a chat."

"I'll make us a couple of pumpkin spice lattes," Kelley volunteered.

"And I'll get the snacks!" I headed to the walk-in cooler and grabbed some "fresh-made" banana bread to thaw. When I came back out, Kelley motioned for me to take a seat while she finished up with the drinks.

"You know," she told me when she came to join me in the lone booth. "My mom told me I was crazy for coming here. For trying to get to know him. I probably should have listened. At least then I'd still be able to imagine what he was like, what he might be doing. Rather than knowing for a fact he was dead."

And so began a very uncomfortable conversation, indeed.

Well, at least it was for me.

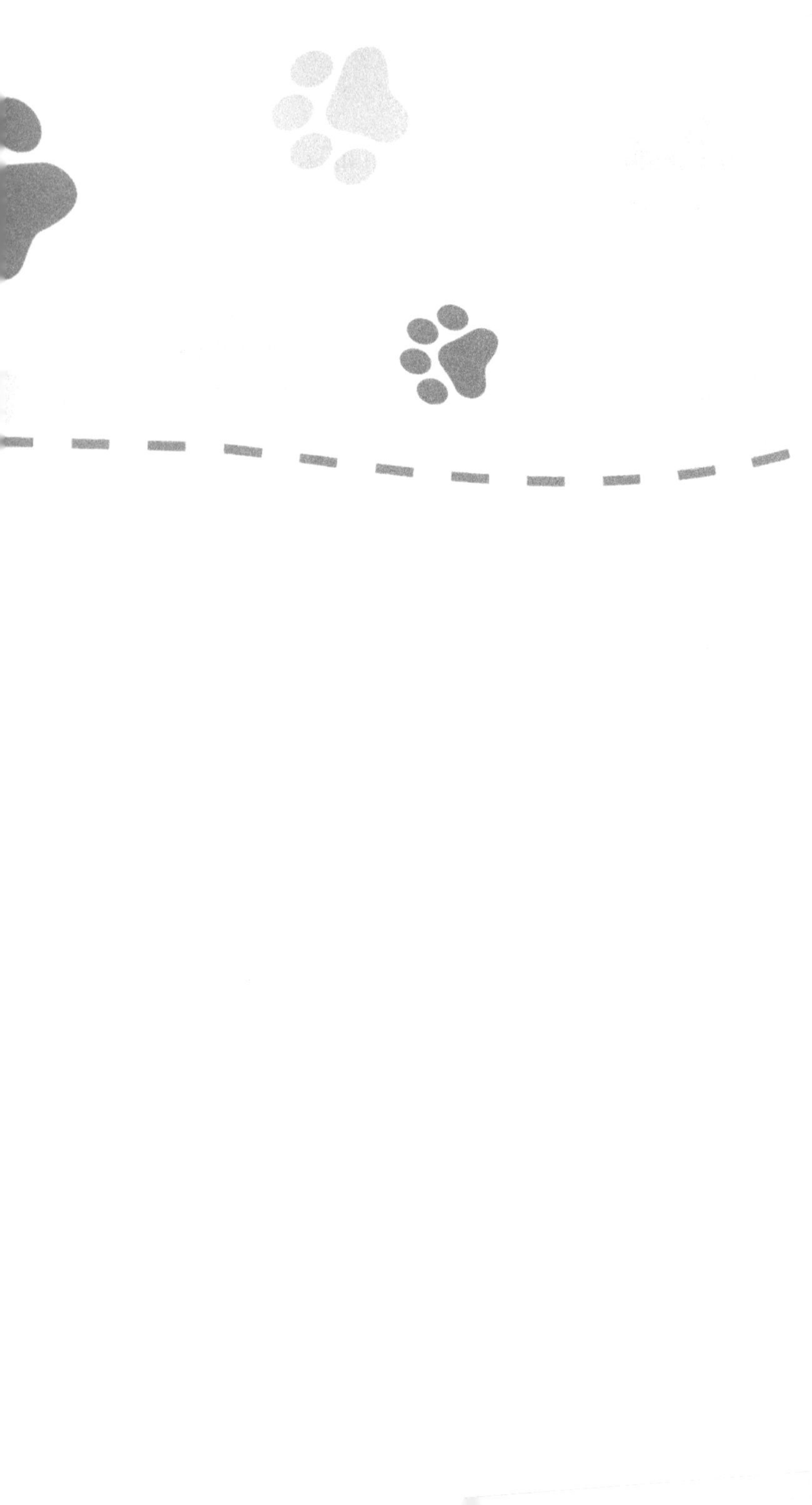

11

pressed my lips in a firm line and nodded as Kelley shared a small glimpse into her family history. The whole purpose of this conversation was for me to help her get to know her late father better, but what if she actually knew more than she realized? What if Kelley had some special glimpse into Harold's life that helped pinpoint his killer?

She'd certainly been paying better attention to his comings and goings than I ever had.

But my young coworker was also already so distraught over his passing, it seemed wrong to push her for information when that could possibly make things worse for her.

And yet if someone didn't find out who actually killed Harold—and soon—I could end up taking the blame. Thinking of it in this way made my path obvious.

I cleared my throat and cast my eyes toward the table. "Did things end on bad terms with your mother and father?" I asked, seeing no other option but to nudge her gently and hope for the best.

Kelley sighed and reached for one of the pieces of banana nut bread, then realizing it was still ice cold, placed it back on the plate and wrapped both hands around her to-go cup. "Mom said if she never saw him again it would still be too soon," she murmured.

"That bad, huh?"

Kelley leaned back against the booth and let her head rest against the worn vinyl cushioning. "Yup."

"Did I ever tell you about the first time I met Harold?"

Kelley shook her head and her eyes widened. "No, but please do."

"Well, I was coming in for my interview. Late. And when I showed up, I found him sitting in the office going over his papers while belting out that one song from Phantom of the Opera."

Kelley sat up straight and actually let out a small chuckle. "No way!"

"Yes, way. And that's not all…"

I shared the few pleasant memories I had of my former boss, and Kelley proved to be a rapt audience. By the time we'd drained our lattes, I'd run out of stories to pass on. Also the banana bread had at long last thawed.

I lifted a piece and nodded to Kelley before taking a huge, delicious bite. Hey, even though it wasn't made fresh, it was still freaking delicious.

"So what do you think you'll do now?" I asked as Kelley picked all the walnuts from her bread and popped them into her mouth one by one.

"My mom's on her way to pick me up and drive me back home," she revealed with a grimace.

"Where's she driving from?" I asked conversationally, although it didn't escape my notice that Kelley seemed unhappy about her mother's impending visit.

"Ohio."

"No way." I reached across the table and lightly slapped her hand. "I'm from Michigan."

"Natural enemies," Kelley teased, referring to our home states' bitter rivalry. In reality, though, us both being from the Midwest meant we had more in common than not.

I wanted to know more about her mother, just in case she was a person of interest in this investigation. But I had to be careful about how hard I pressed. Hopefully the light playful moment would help me get further with my next line of questioning. Again, the next to last thing I wanted to do was kick Kelley when she was down. The very last thing I wanted to do was go to jail for a crime I had no hand in committing.

"Your mom must be happy that you're coming back home. Huh?" I ventured, licking my thumb and then pressing it into the crumbs that lay scattered on my plate.

"Yeah." Kelley said, finally taking a proper bite of her dessert. "Like I said, she never wanted me to come in the first place. She said the only good thing my dad had ever done in his whole life was to give her me." She smiled shyly.

"Why'd they break up? Did she ever say?"

"She didn't want to spoil my impression of him. Kind of ironic, huh? She said just to take her at her word and be careful."

That reminded me of rule number two of being

Merlin's familiar: Do whatever he says without asking any questions.

"I know things didn't end well, but I think it's really good you got the chance to meet him," I offered with a small smile.

Kelley sniffed and shook her head. "I don't know."

"You'll get there," I said as if speaking from experience.

"You're probably right." She shrugged and leaned back in the booth, eyes closed. "It's just still all fresh and new, and I'm not sure I can handle my mom trash-talking him before he's even laid to rest."

"Yeah, that's hard." Suddenly I got an idea that could help both of us. "Tell you what, if she gives you any trouble, come see me. Tell her we already had plans before this all happened. I can serve as a buffer."

Kelley opened her eyes and stared at me in silent shock before saying, "Wow. Thank you, Gracie. You are being so nice."

"You deserve a friend right now, and I'm willing to bet you need one, too." I pushed my phone across the table toward her. "Here, enter your phone number, and I'll text you my address."

Kellie grabbed at it eagerly and began to type. As she did, a knock sounded on the door to the coffee shop.

I glanced over and immediately recognized the silhouette of the last person I wanted to see just then.

Officer Dash had come to pay us a visit.

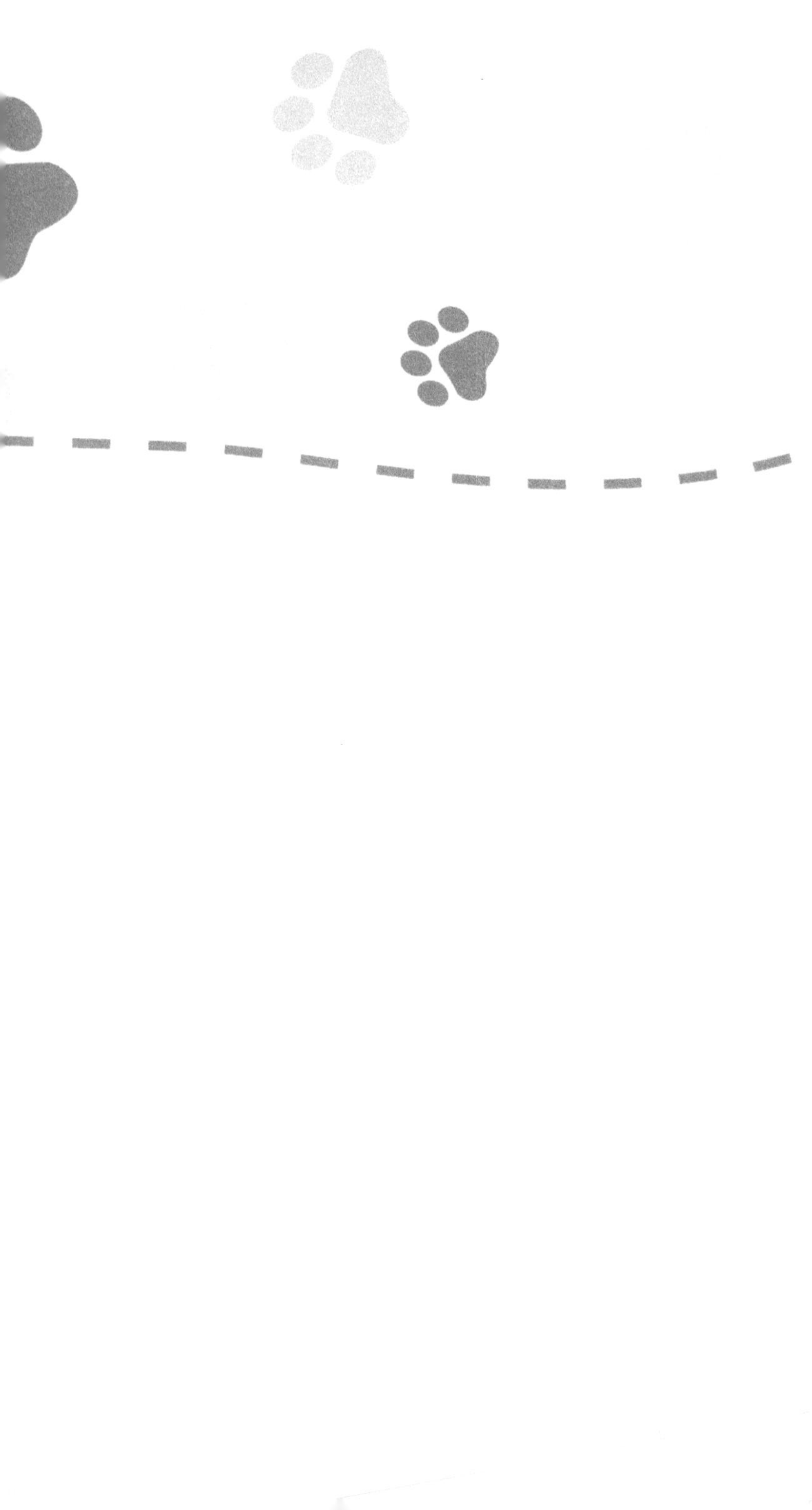

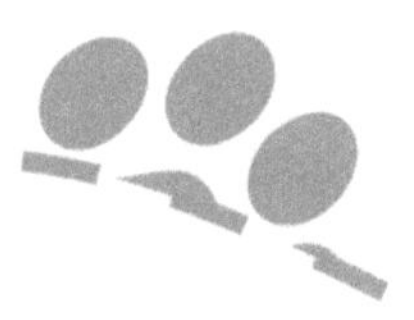

12

As soon as we heard the knocking, Kelley immediately jumped up to let the police-woman inside.

Officer Dash smirked when she saw me. "Figures you'd be here, exactly where you aren't supposed to be."

"We were scheduled to work today," Kelley explained, jumping straight to my rescue. Now that I was getting to know her better, I really did like her.

"Well, sorry to say, this place of business is closed until further notice." Dash didn't look sorry, though. Not one bit.

"Do you have any idea when that might be?" I asked, gathering the two empty plates and taking them back to the small sink we used to keep things tidy.

Dash's eyes followed me, tracing every movement. "Not until we conclude our investigation and Harris's attorney settles his estate."

"Do you happen to know who's handling his will?" Kelley asked, tucking her hair behind each ear and glancing down. Well, at least I wasn't the only person intimidated by the brusque policewoman. Still, this was the last thing that poor Kelley needed right now.

"That's private family business," Officer Dash snapped, only glancing toward Kelly for a moment before staring me down again.

"I know," Kelley mumbled as she studied her shoes. "I'm his daughter."

"If you're meant to be included, his attorney will contact you," the officer explained with a hard gaze. "How come you didn't disclose your relationship with the deceased the first time we talked?"

Kelley shook her head. "I'm still coming to terms with all of this."

"They were estranged," I piped up. "Until very recently."

"Interesting." Officer Dash pulled out that little steno notebook of hers and jotted a few things down. "Do you mind accompanying me to the station for a few questions?"

Kelley's eyes widened in horror.

"Is that really necessary?" I argued, moving in front of Kelley protectively. "Can't you see how upset she already is?"

"Oh, did I hurt your little friend's feelings?" she asked with a cruel smile. "Silly me, I was just trying to bring a murderer to justice here!"

Officer Dash stomped her foot, and Kelley's trembling fingers reached for my arm.

I turned to face my frightened young colleague. "You didn't do anything wrong, which means you've got nothing to hide. Even this one is going to see that," I said, hooking a thumb back toward a very cranky Officer Dash.

"Stay?" Kelley begged.

"I really need to question each suspect separately," the policewoman informed us.

Kelley gasped. "Suspect?"

"Look, she's a little rough around the edges—okay, a lot. But she can't do a thing to you. You have my number now, call me anytime you need me. Any reason."

Kelley nodded, and I stepped aside.

"Ever ridden in the back of a cop car before?"

Officer Dash asked with a bemused expression, sending Kelley shrinking back.

"Enough," I growled. As soon as this investigation was over, I would be filing a big fat complaint about Officer Dash's lack of professionalism. Anonymously, of course.

"You can talk here," I continued. "I'll leave to give you both some privacy."

I squeezed Kelley's hand and told her it would be okay, then saw myself out. Neither of them tried to stop me.

I waited in the parking lot for a few minutes just to make sure Officer Dash wasn't honestly planning on carting the poor aggrieved daughter to the station for an interrogation.

Once I was satisfied that she wasn't, I began the short drive home.

In my distracted state, I almost ran a red light and drove up over the curb more than once. Why did Officer Dash have to be so combative about the investigation? Moreover, why had she come into the coffeehouse that afternoon? Had she been looking for me?

I worried now that if they didn't find the real killer soon, Officer Dash might even stoop to fabricating evidence just so she could close the investigation and move on.

Scary.

Maybe I should file that complaint against her sooner than later...

One more chance, I decided as I pulled into my driveway. One more encounter. If Officer Dash didn't start behaving more professionally with her very next visit, I would be heading into the station to discuss matters with her boss.

That small thing decided, I pushed my car into park, took a deep breath, and headed inside to see what new trouble my cat had gotten us into during my brief absence.

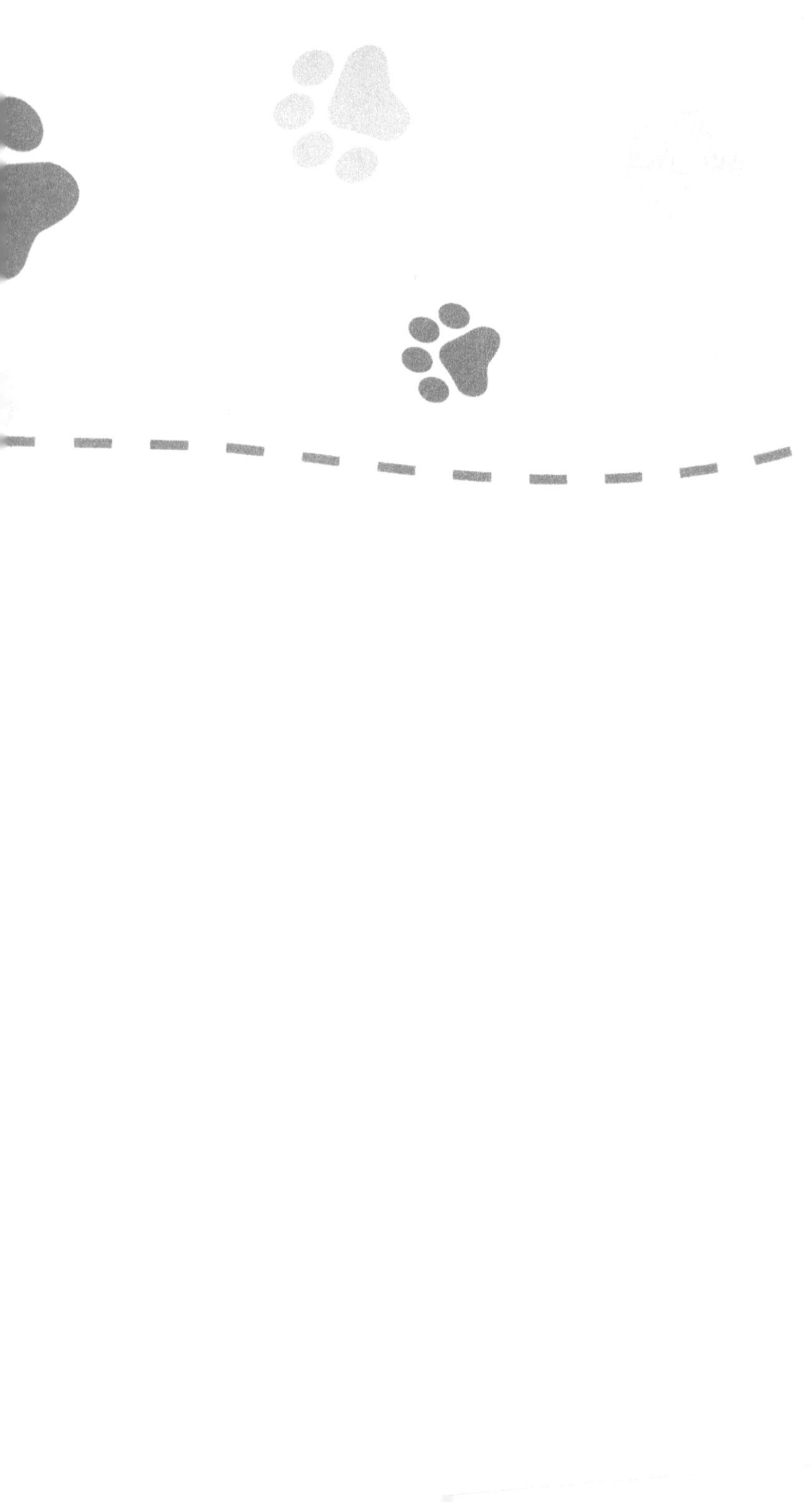

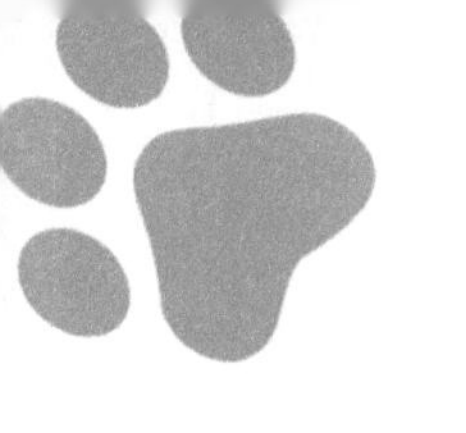

13

crept into the house, not sure what I would find. Merlin had been alone for almost two hours, thanks to my strange shift at work. Funny, I'd never had to worry about what he did while I was away before. Now all I did was worry... about him, about Harold, about life on the whole.

Well, whatever he had gotten up to in my absence, it hadn't caused any obvious damage. In fact, the house was exactly as I'd left it. Even Luna's journal still lay open on the couch, exactly as it had been when we'd reviewed it together earlier. He must have taken it, and then brought it back. But why?

"Merlin?" I called as I moved toward the couch and peered down at the filched object. The two-page spread on display was filled with furious illegible scrawl, and I couldn't make any sense of it.

Yeesh. I'd hoped he would have returned his nemesis's journal when he was done with it, or at the very least hid it somewhere. It was like he was courting trouble here and doing it on purpose.

I took a quick picture of the journal's pages on my cell phone, then grabbed it up and headed out to return it myself.

Problem was, I didn't know exactly how to get to Luna's cottage, seeing as we'd teleported there and back, but I remembered seeing the crossroads at the edge of the property when we escaped. One of the roads was called Persimmon. I typed the street and city name into my phone's GPS and got directions to the general location. Thank goodness for modern technology.

Persimmon lay on the other side of town, but still it only took me ten minutes to find Luna's home and park outside. I tucked the journal into my purse and moved toward the door.

An older woman answered before I even had the chance to knock.

"Hello. Virginia?" I asked hopefully.

"Gracie," she answered with a sigh, then stepped back and allowed me to enter.

Good. This was good.

Now I just had to find a way to return the journal without her noticing I'd taken it in the first place.

So I put on my best, most cordial smile, and said, "I just wanted to stop by and introduce myself. I know our cats are fighting, but I see no reason why we can't get along."

Although she was much older than me, Virginia seemed to possess a grace and easiness within herself that I'd never known. Her blonde hair was an obvious dye job even though I couldn't see any dark roots peeking through, and her green eyes studied me with a quiet intelligence I found comforting.

"Would you like some sweet tea?" Virginia offered, gliding toward the kitchen.

"Please." I knew it would rude not to accept, but also kind of stupid to actually drink anything she gave me, given that I didn't know if we were on good terms. Still, I liked her, despite Merlin's warnings. There was something I instantly related to, although I couldn't say what. Maybe we familiars had more in common than just our job. I thought about all this as I stood waiting awkwardly near the door.

Virginia cracked a tray of ice cubes and dropped several into each of two glasses.

Focus. I needed to focus. Remember the purpose for this visit.

Hmmm. Could I just stick the journal on the entry table and call it good?

No, no. Too obvious.

"Come. Let's have a seat." Virginia guided me to the tacky floral couch I'd spotted on my first visit, and we both settled in with our sweet tea. She smiled warmly at me as if we were old friends and not new acquaintances.

I placed my purse on the floor by my feet. When she wasn't looking, I could take the journal out and kick it beneath the couch for them to find later. I just had to wait for my opportunity.

"You're still very new," Virginia pointed out. When I looked at her askance, she added, "To the familiar life."

I bobbed my head and pretended to take a sip from my glass.

Virginia's casual smile faded at once. Even the soothing green of her eyes appeared to sharpen in an instant. "Our witches' feuds are ours, too. We don't have any autonomy in their world. So if our cats are fighting, then we are, too."

I coughed and set my sweet tea on the coffee table. It seemed there was no need to keep up appearances if she was going to wear her hostility on her sleeve here.

"Are you sure?" I asked with a frown. "It just seems so silly. Shouldn't we witches and familiars stick together?"

"That's not our decision. Now that we've met, I hope you're satisfied. You may finish your tea and leave." Virginia drained hers in a single gulp, then wandered off down the hallway and let herself into a private room.

I had to act fast. Something told me if I wasn't gone by the time Virginia came back, I might not be able to get away. How quickly she had transformed. This frightened me. Would I one day become like her, too? Was this the life my witchy cat had cursed me to live in choosing me as his familiar?

Desperate to get out of there and fast, I knocked my purse onto its side with my heel, trying to make it look like an accident in case anyone was watching. Then I bent down and grabbed it, taking care to shove the journal as far back as I could.

Satisfied with my work, I took my still full beverage to the kitchen and dumped it down the sink drain, then let myself out into the yard and bolted for my waiting car.

So much for diplomacy.

Whatever our cats' problem with each other, the two felines would just have to find a way to work it out for themselves.

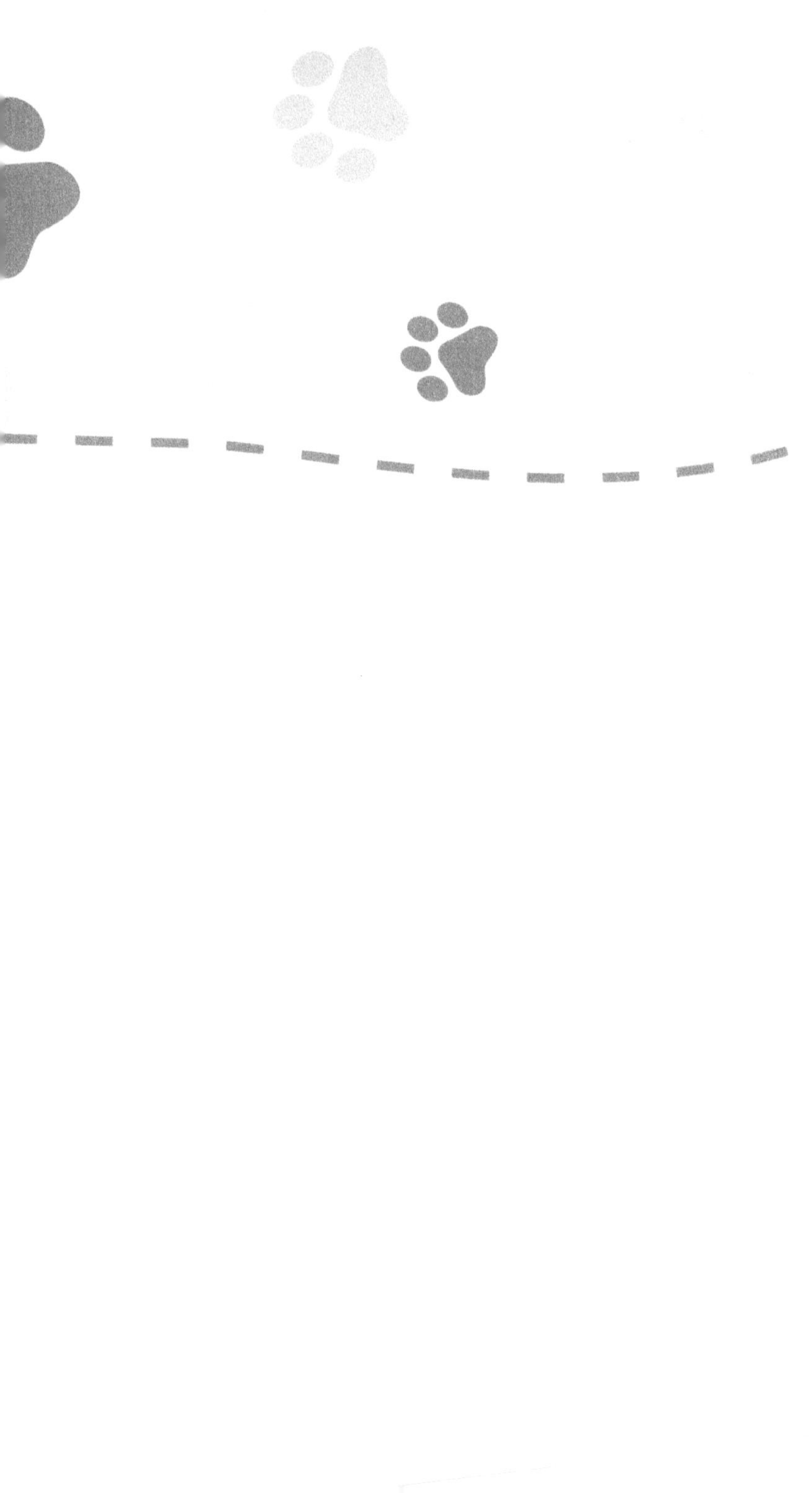

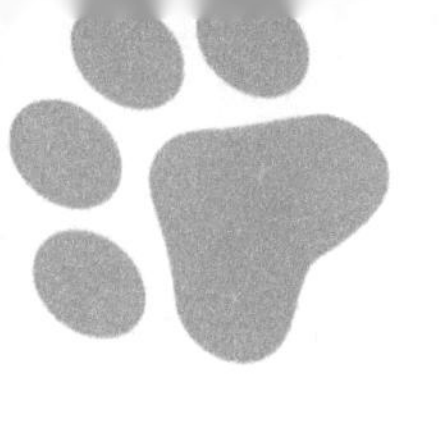

14

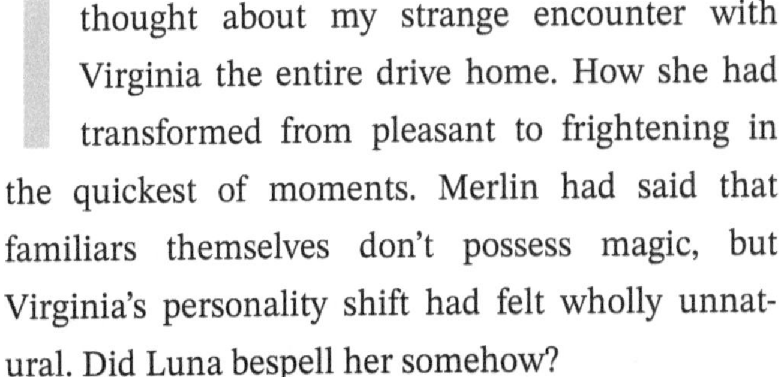

thought about my strange encounter with Virginia the entire drive home. How she had transformed from pleasant to frightening in the quickest of moments. Merlin had said that familiars themselves don't possess magic, but Virginia's personality shift had felt wholly unnatural. Did Luna bespell her somehow?

And, more importantly, would Merlin do something similar to me?

I didn't like this one bit. Was it too late for me to tell him "thanks, but no thanks" and leave him to find someone better suited to lifelong magical servitude?

I had a feeling that no matter where I ran to, Merlin would find me and drag me back. And other than being a little rude, he hadn't done a single thing to hurt me. In fact, he'd promised to protect me, at least when it came to Harold's murder investigation.

Whatever the case, he and I clearly needed to have a long talk before he asked anything more of me. Lesson two said that I was supposed to trust him, but he needed to trust me, too. And he needed to offer some kind of guidebook into my new life if he expected me to assimilate.

Yes, we would have a nice long chat, provided I could find him. I took a deep breath and pushed open the door to my home, more than ready for a heart-to-heart.

But I didn't find Merlin waiting for me.

Instead, the house had been ransacked during my brief visit with Virginia. I'd only been gone half an hour, tops, but cushions had been torn off the couch, chairs overturned, the whole nine yards.

Thinking fast, I grabbed a broom from the front closet and proceeded deeper into my house with the end raised like a baseball bat.

"Who's there?" I called as my eyes darted all around. Who would burgle me in broad daylight? And why? I didn't have anything good.

Suddenly the broom flew from my hands and whipped back around to pin me against the wall.

"Where is it?" a lanky white cat demanded, tiptoeing toward me. *Luna.*

"Let me go," I cried, struggling against the broom, but Luna's magic proved stronger than my muscles.

"Not until you tell me where it is!" She stopped about a foot in front of me and unsheathed the claws on one paw. "Tell me right now!"

I could play dumb and pretend I didn't know what she was talking about, but it seemed easier to give in to her demands. "The journal?" I asked.

Her glowing green eyes widened. "So you admit to the theft?"

"I admit I took it, but I also brought it right back. I'm sorry."

"You have no idea what you've done. What trouble you've caused."

"Again, I'm really sorry. Please let me go?" I begged meekly.

"No," she told me with a beastly growl. "You started this, and you'll be the one to finish it."

The broom dropped, and I lurched forward. No sooner had I been freed than one of my wooden dining chairs slammed into me from behind. I fell into a sitting position and then the broom pressed me against the chair, securing me in place.

"Please..." I cried actual tears now. "I never asked to become Merlin's familiar. I never asked for any of this."

"You're coming with me," Luna said, then blinked once, twice...

And we were back at her cottage. "Are you going to kill me now?"

"Where's the journal?" Luna hissed, ignoring my desperate question.

"Under the c-c-couch," I sputtered, seeing no point in lying now.

The thin cat ran beneath the couch, then came out with the notebook gripped between her jaws.

I remained stuck in the chair, only able to watch as she levitated the book to the coffee table and flipped through its pages.

Apparently having found what she was looking for, she smiled, blinked, and took us into her rear garden. Then she approached an old stone wall, dragging me along with her magic.

"What are you doing?" I ground out.

"That doesn't concern you." Luna hopped onto my lap and pawed at my pants, picking something up and dropping it into the well.

Then she ran back and chomped at my hair, ran back to the well, and spit inside.

"Is that your cauldron?" I guessed.

"Ah, so he has taught you something, at least. Not enough to keep you from playing right into my paw, though."

"What? I don't understand."

"Good, then your boss won't see it coming, either."

"What are you plotting?"

"Nothing that concerns you. I'm just setting things right," she said, walking through her garden and plucking various leaves and petals to drop into the well.

I watched her work for at least twenty minutes, but nothing I said could convince her to tell me anything more. Sometime later, a shimmering emerald puff rose from the well and Luna laughed girlishly rather than wickedly.

"Purrfect," she exclaimed. "Now return home and mix this in your master's water dish." She pushed an empty plastic bottle into the well with her paw. And when she brought it back up with her magic, it held a small amount of liquid. No more than half an inch deep.

"I won't do it," I said, struggling against the broom and chair once more.

Luna laughed again as the broom snapped away and the chair crumbled into a pile of sawdust. "Funny thing is, you don't have a choice. And you won't be able to warn him, either. It's brewed right into the spell."

"That's why you took my hair," I realized.

"Yes. And his. It's lucky for me he sheds so much and can't resist a warm lap, eh?"

"I don't know what you're planning, but you won't get away with it."

"I already have," Luna said with a smirk.

She blinked once, twice...

And I was back home with the water bottle clutched firmly in my hand. Before I could stop myself, I poured its contents into Merlin's bowl. As soon as I did, the plastic container dissolved into thin air and completely disappeared.

No, no, no! I strained for his dish, but something yanked me back. I couldn't stop whatever Luna had planned from happening, and I couldn't find Merlin anywhere to keep an eye on the situation.

What now?

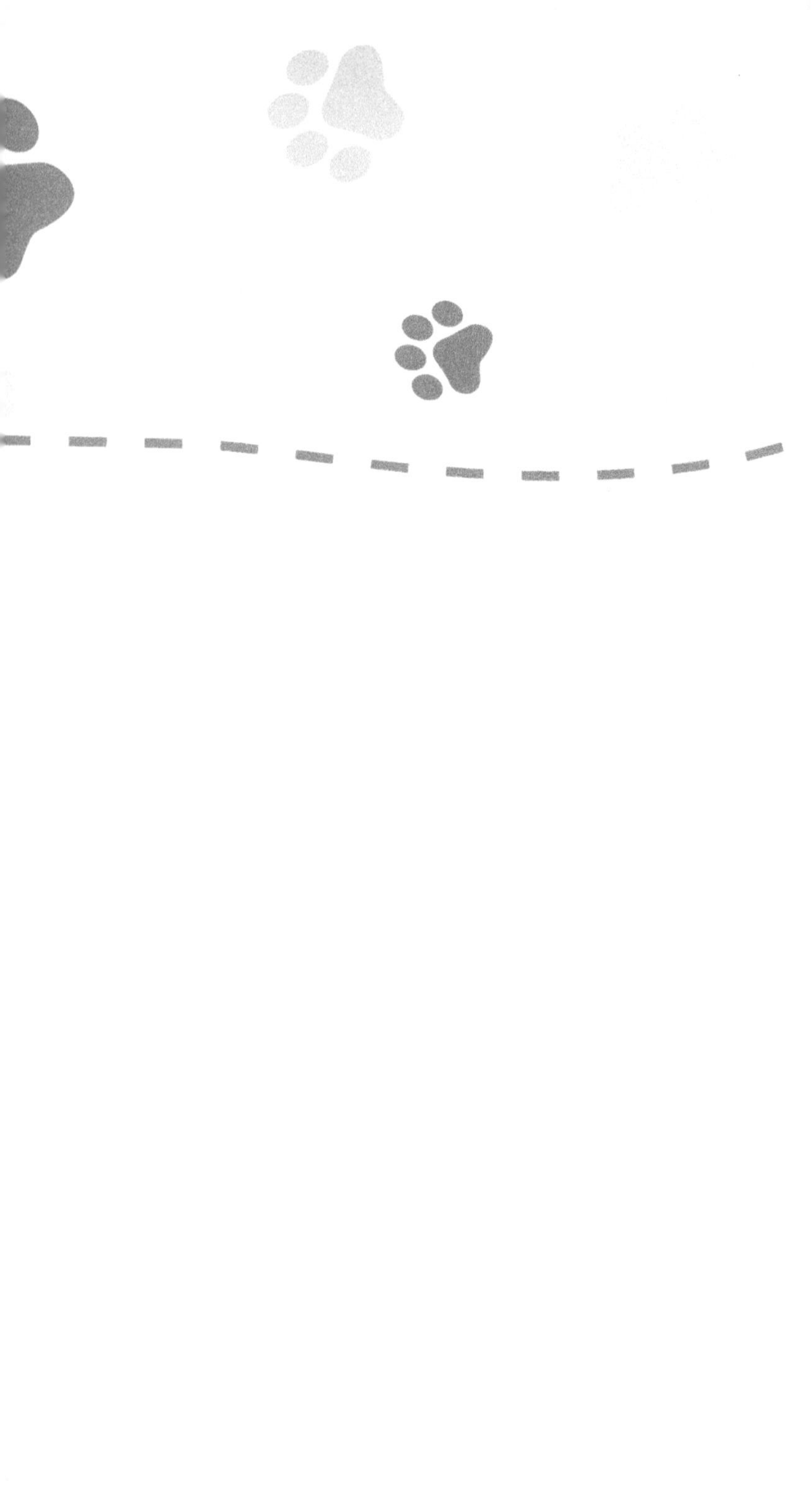

15

I must have fallen asleep at some point, because the next thing I knew the sun had crept between my bedroom blinds and was now beaming directly into my eyes.

Merlin jumped onto my chest and brushed his fluffy tail in my face. "You sleep a lot for a human. Are you sure you're not part cat?" he quipped. A wry smile stretched between his bright white whiskers.

And that was when everything came rushing back—Luna, the potion, my part in it all.

"Merlin!" I cried and hugged him hard against my chest. "You're okay!"

He struggled from my grip and then jumped out of reach, looking at me like I was crazy. "Of course

I'm okay. Why wouldn't I be okay?" His fur twitched in odd spasms across his back, a sure sign I'd overstepped my bounds as a cat owner.

"Because I—" I began, but my words were abruptly cut off.

"Well, yester—" I tried again. "L—"

Each time I tried to speak, I found myself gagged mid-sentence.

"You're being weird," my cat said, his ears pressed back against his head.

And he was right; I was being weird. I also didn't know how to stop. Maybe if I tried talking about something else...

"Want breakfast?" I asked casually, and sure enough, that I could get out without being magically silenced. Whatever Luna had worked into her spell, it seemed impossible for me to get around it.

Perhaps if I had more knowledge or guidance, I'd be able to find a way... but only Merlin could give me answers, and I wasn't even able to ask him any of the right questions.

"Yes, I want breakfast. Do you even need to ask?" Merlin hopped off the bed and slipped through the doorway.

Worry gnawed at my brain as I followed.

In the kitchen, I found that his water dish had

been licked dry. I wanted to ask how he was feeling after lapping up Luna's potion, but couldn't. So I simply shook my head and refilled his dish from the tap.

"Are you going into work today?" Merlin asked as I opened a can of wet food and plopped it in his bowl.

"Not today."

"Good. We can continue your training." His piece said, Merlin turned his attentions toward his breakfast.

Biding my time until Luna's spell activated proved to be complete agony. I was glad that everything appeared normal thus far today, but waiting for the other shoe to drop made it hard to focus on anything else.

"Aren't you going to make some coffee?" Merlin asked me some time later.

I glanced toward his bowl and saw he'd already polished off his breakfast. Wow, I must have been lost in space for the last few minutes.

"Yes, coffee," I said, not unlike a zombie as I made my way to the Keurig to brew some liquid energy.

"Lesson number three," Merlin announced from his spot on the linoleum kitchen floor. "In all things you do, you are a representative of me. If you do something good, I will receive the praise. If you do something bad, I will receive the punishment."

"Why are you telling me this?" I asked nervously.

He stared at me unblinking, unmoving even. "So you don't mess up."

I gulped hard. I'd already messed up and messed up big, but I also had no way of telling him that. Shoot.

"You are not magical," he continued, unaware of my raging internal conflict. "But you are a reservoir. Kind of like a living, breathing cauldron. Your presence amplifies my magic. The longer we spend in each other's company, the more of my magic will bind to you. You can't use it for yourself. Only contain it for my later use."

Now this was a big revelation, far too big for me to understand pre-coffee.

Merlin hopped up on the counter and studied my face. "In fact, it seems you've already collected some," he said.

"What?" I croaked, lifting my fingers to my face.

My cat smirked. "Your eyes."

"What about my eyes?"

"Stop panicking and go have a look."

I marched toward the bathroom and flicked on the light. Instead of my usual dark brown, my eyes now appeared a deep forest green.

"Green!" I shouted, unable to believe the image that floated right before me. "Why are my eyes green?"

"Well, that's easy," Merlin said, appearing in the hall outside the bathroom. "Eyes are the window to the soul. Green is the color of magic. Now you are magic, thus your soul is tinted green."

"You said I wasn't magical," I argued hopelessly. It was really hard to trust everything he said when so much of it seemed contradictory.

Merlin yawned and stretched out in a yoga-like pose. "You're not *magical.* You are magic. It's a subtle distinction, but you'll get it eventually," he assured me.

Either Merlin had faith in me or was too stubborn to admit he'd been wrong in choosing me as his familiar. And at that precise moment in time, I really didn't care to know which.

Ugh. Why was this my life?

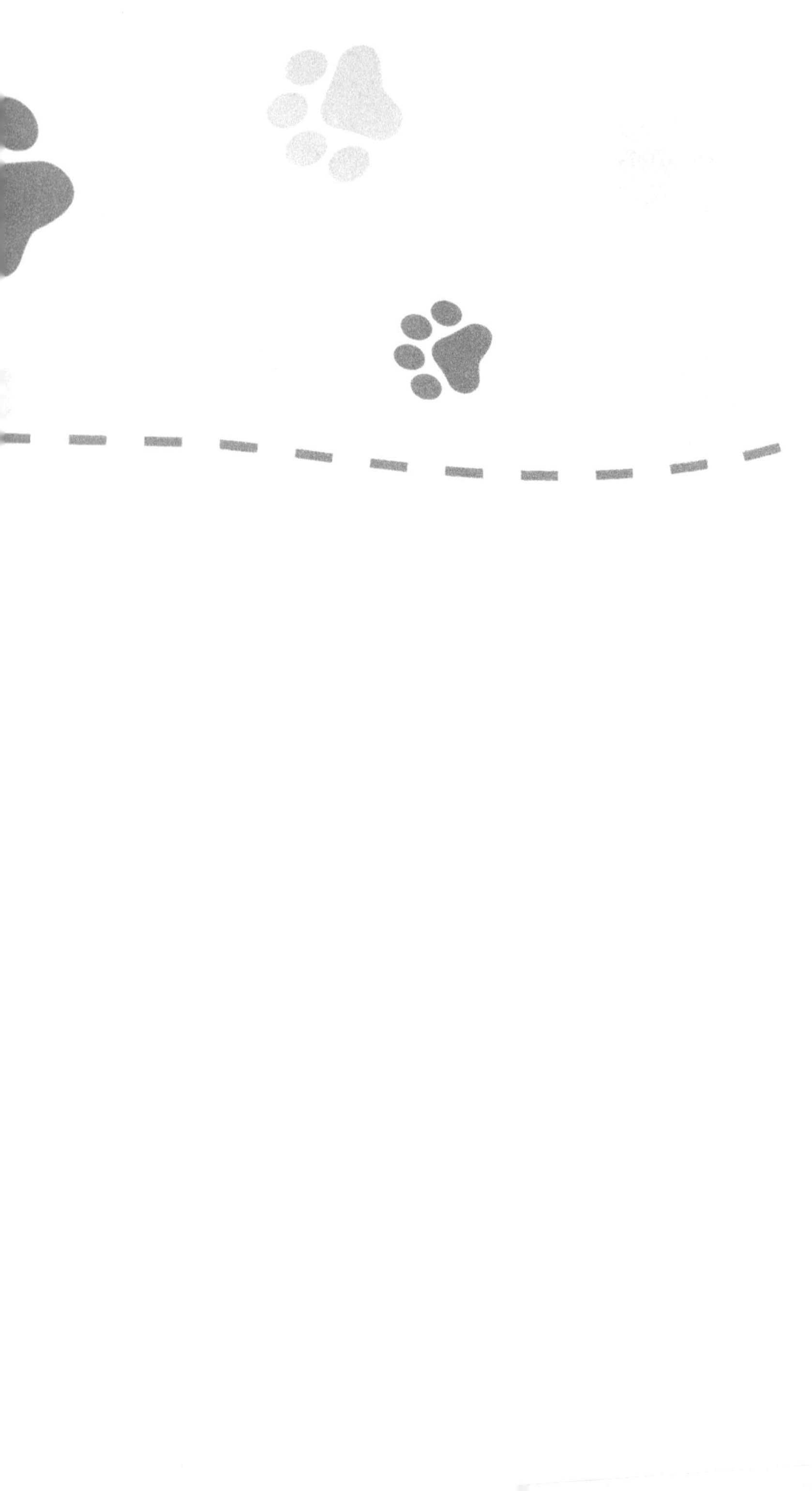

16

still hoped to speak with Merlin about Luna, but my magic bindings shut me down every single time I even thought about it too hard.

To avoid wasting time completely, I decided to ask him about something much safer—the open murder investigation.

"Merlin?" I asked as my second cuppa brewed. "Can you use your magic to find out who killed Harold?"

He thought about this for a moment as he shifted to follow the sunbeam that had slowly begun to migrate across the living room. "Possibly. But I would need to see his corpse to do so."

I shuddered. "Let's make breaking into the

morgue our backup plan," I suggested, wrapping my arms around my torso to hug myself.

"Suit yourself," Merlin responded, then closed his eyes and purred. "If you do end up needing me, you know where to find me."

Yes, I did. For right now, at least. His constant coming and going hadn't bothered me much before. But now? Now every time we were apart presented another opportunity for one of us to be kidnapped.

Oh, if only I could warn him.

I knew he had just recently been made a full witch—something he said only happened when a cat officially took on a familiar. But still it seemed his casual attitude could be putting us both in danger. I, of course, was even newer to the whole magical powers thing, which meant he had no reason to listen to me if I asked for better protection.

And seeing as I couldn't come right out and explain why I needed that protection, we were both stuck.

I sighed and added some milk to my new cup of coffee and stirred while I mentally sorted through what I already knew about my late boss's death. It would be easier to focus on my magical problems if I got my more mundane ones out of the way.

Of course, I hadn't ever conversed with Harold outside of work, and it was perfectly probable that some scandal in his personal life had led to his forced demise. Given my butt was on the line here, though, it made sense to at least consider the clues I'd picked up.

First, there was the fact that his long-lost daughter Kelley had recently reappeared in his life. And that Kelley's mother had tried to prevent this reunion. Kelley was also present when Harold took his last breath, but she was too obviously distraught to even be considered a suspect.

Drake had been there, too. Come to think of it, I hadn't seen him since. Was it possible he hated our boss so much that he'd slipped him some poison?

I'd definitely have to look into that later.

The coffee house had been mostly empty besides the three of us and Harold. Only one customer had sat in the corner sipping her coffee, and she'd left as soon as we asked her to.

Hmmm.

Another thing to consider was that the poison could have been meant for me, and Harold was merely collateral damage. The more I thought about it, the more I feared this could be the case. I'd only just witnessed Merlin's magic for the first time before rushing into work. That had been a test, he'd told me, to see if I was ready to serve as his familiar. Then later that night he had revealed himself to me.

I already knew he had an enemy in Luna, and she lived very nearby. She was also crazy enough to kidnap me and brew some kind of voodoo potion, which she forced me to slip to my cat last night.

Was this because her first attempt to get at me had failed when Harold took the poison instead?

Officer Dash had hinted at a toxicology report but never shared the results. Had it been completed? Did we know for sure we were dealing with a poison—or could some kind of magic be at play?

So many questions, and literally no one to ask. Maybe if I was careful about how I spoke with Merlin, I could suss out some answers about Luna indirectly. I finished my coffee and lowered myself to sit beside him on the living room carpet.

"Do you have any idea who might have killed Harold?" I asked him softly.

Merlin kept his eyes closed, but his whiskers twitched, telling me he had heard my question but didn't much like it. "Do you want to break into the morgue?"

I shivered at the thought. "Can you go without me?" I asked, preferring that option much more. "Just teleport in, check things out, and come back."

"I could," he said, squinting one eye open to look at me. "Except I don't know which one is him."

Crud. I really didn't want to go sift through a bunch of cold corpses, but I also really didn't want to go to jail. Could I suck it up for the greater good?

"Got a picture?" Merlin asked, rolling onto his feet and standing on four shaky legs.

Ooh, a picture. Smart! Why hadn't I thought of that?

"Let me search the coffeehouse's Facebook page. I'm sure there's at least one useable shot there," I told him and then trotted off in search of my tablet.

Why hadn't we thought of this option sooner?

Well, better late than never, I supposed…

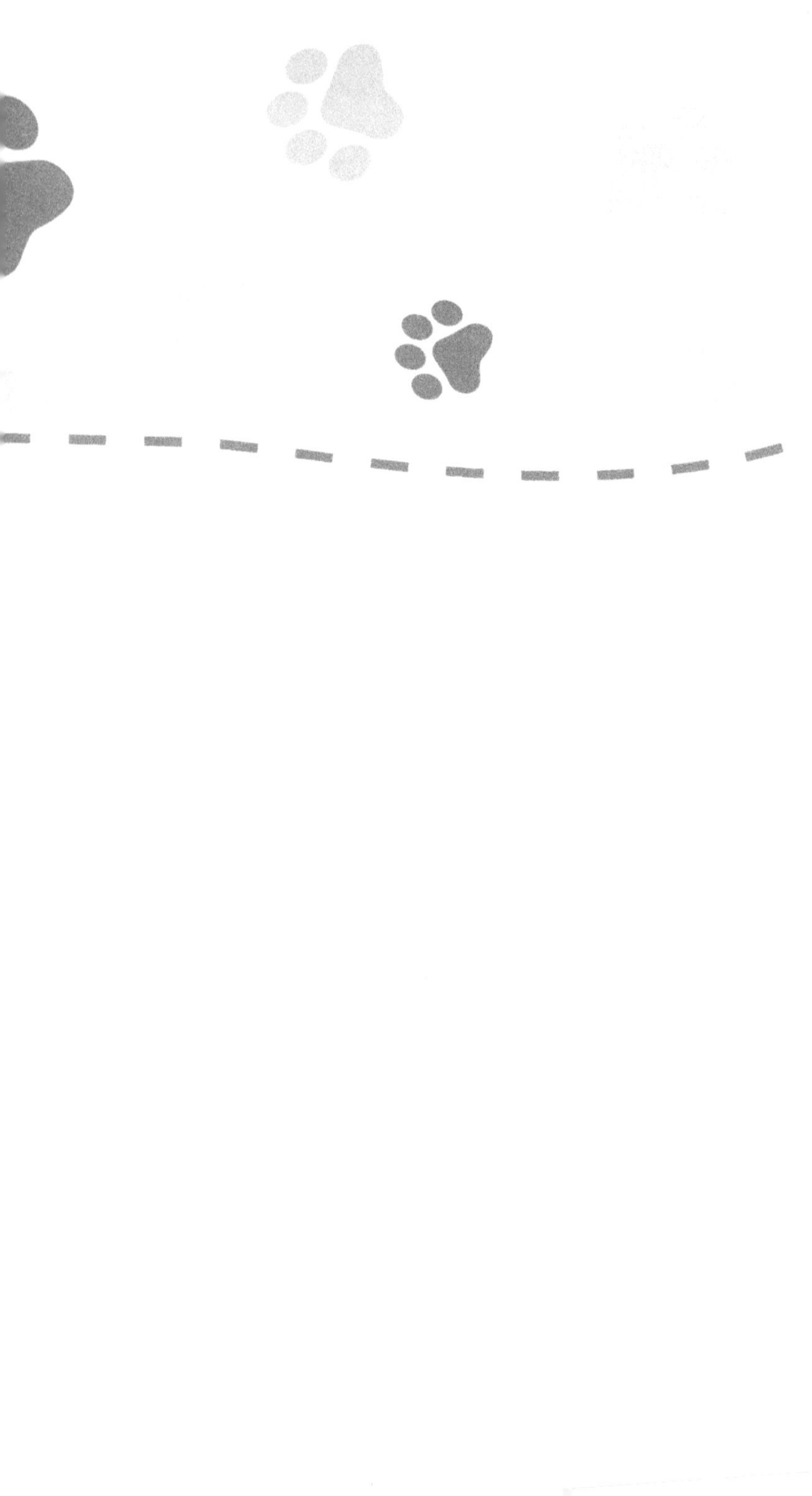

17

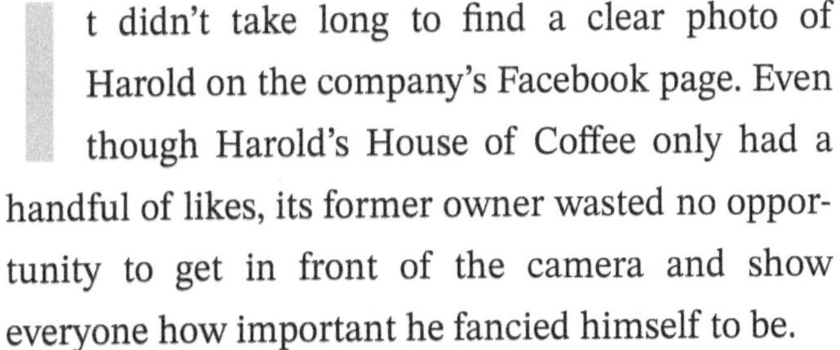

t didn't take long to find a clear photo of Harold on the company's Facebook page. Even though Harold's House of Coffee only had a handful of likes, its former owner wasted no opportunity to get in front of the camera and show everyone how important he fancied himself to be.

"I can work with this," Merlin informed me when I shared the image with him. "I can't teleport directly into the morgue, so this little fact-finding mission may take me a while."

"Why can't you?" I asked, uneasy at the thought of being away from him—and his magical protections—for an extended period.

"Same reason I took us outside of Luna's house, then flashed us in through the window. If you're going someplace you can't see and don't know well, you risk getting yourself stuck in a wall or in some other precarious situation," the novice feline witch explained.

"Oh," I said stupidly.

"Lesson number four. Magic is much harder to wield than it may look to outsiders," he announced and cracked his neck to either side.

"I'm beginning to see that."

A knock sounded on the front door, and I briefly glanced over to it. By the time I turned back to Merlin, he had already vanished.

I groaned and headed to find out what Officer Dash wanted. Because, yes, I already knew it would be her. She'd bothered me so much the past couple of days that I readily recognized the unique cadence of her knock.

Bang. Bang. Tap, tap, tap. BANG!

I flung the door open, reminding myself that if she didn't behave more professionally in this exchange, I'd be taking a trip to the station to issue a formal complaint. That at least brought me some satisfaction as I came face-to-face with my current least favorite person in all the world.

"The toxicology report came back," Officer Dash

informed me as she hooked a finger into her belt loop.

I crossed my arms and remained planted in the doorway, not allowing her into my house. "And?"

Officer Dash hooked her other thumb in her belt loop and rocked back on her heels. "Gas Line Antifreeze. Not something most people need for a summer in Elderberry Heights. Say, you're from up north, right?"

"Michigan," I managed as my stomach roiled. "What's your point?"

"And is that your car in the driveway there?"

"Yeah." I definitely did not like where this was headed.

"Huh," the policewoman said simply.

"C'mon. You can't honestly think that this proves anything! Antifreeze is readily available. Even here in Southern Georgia, I'm sure."

Out came that stupid notebook of hers. "*Uh-huh. Uh-huh.* And how do you happen to know that?"

"I didn't kill Harold," I said between gritted teeth.

"Sure, you didn't." She smiled. "I'll be back with a search warrant. Oh, and I wouldn't leave town if I were you."

Fantastic.

I slammed the door shut as soon as Officer Dash sauntered away. She looked like the cat who was about to eat the canary, so happy with her upcoming kill she couldn't see anything else... Like the fact that I was not guilty!

My phone buzzed in my pocket, and I took it out to find a next text from Kelley.

I told my mom I'd be meeting you for lunch. She insisted on coming along.

Hmm. So Kelley's mom was now in town and causing problems for her.

Where? I texted back.

The BBQ Shack at 12.

I'll be there.

I still thought Officer Dash was grasping at straws, but if her antifreeze theory played out, then I knew at least one other potential suspect who'd come from colder climates.

And I was about to have lunch with her.

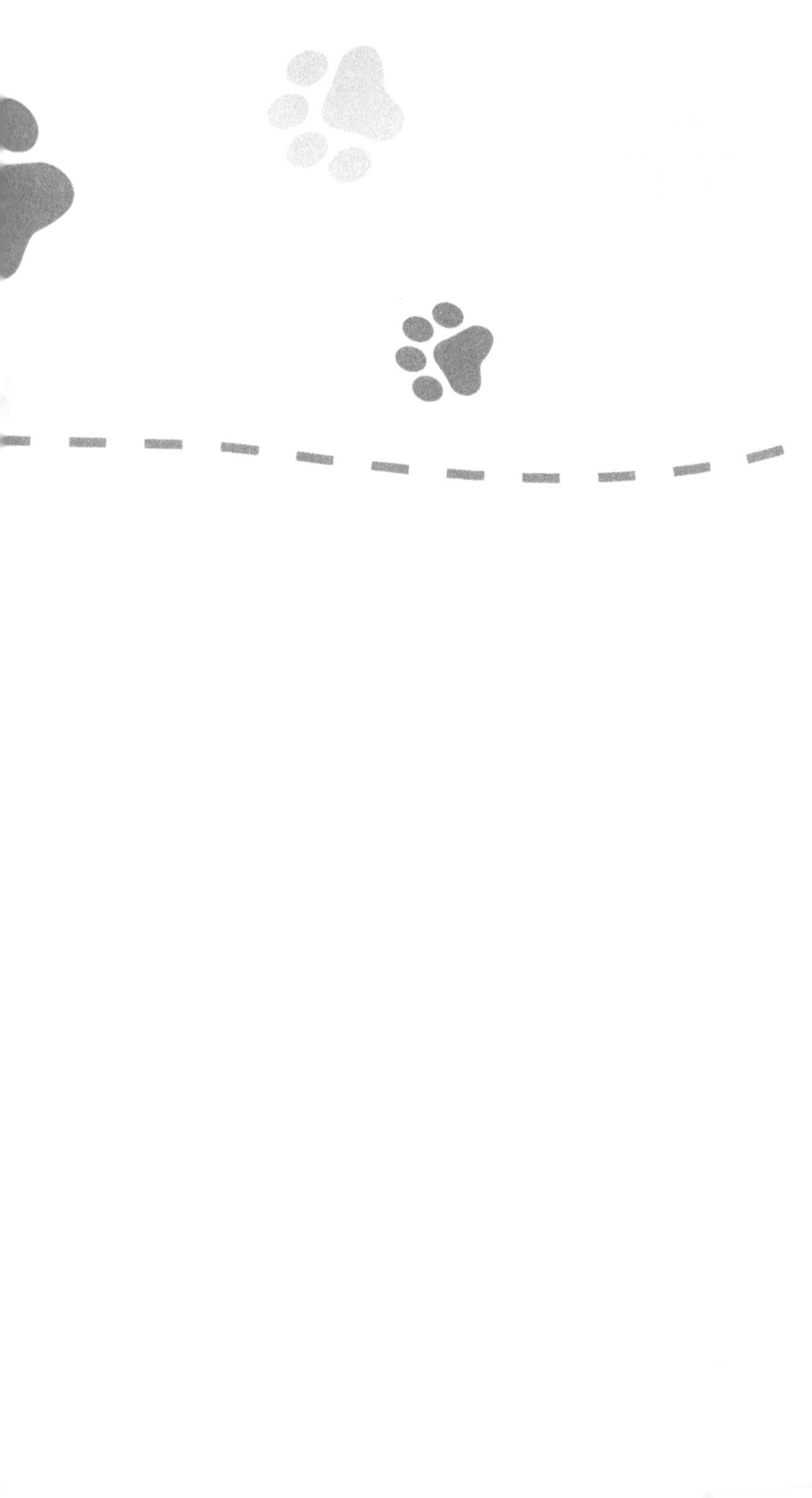

18

Despite my ardent hope, Merlin didn't return before I had to leave for my impromptu lunch date. I wished I could call him back now that Officer Dash had told me the exact cause of death, but unfortunately I had no way of getting in touch with him.

He'd find out soon enough, I supposed. And I could rest a little easier knowing that our dear Harold hadn't been killed by magical means.

I applied my normal going-out face of makeup. Then, hating what I saw, I washed my whole face clean. The striking blue eyeshadow I normally wore to complement my dark brown eyes appeared clownish when paired with my new forest green irises. I'd have to add a trip to the drugstore cosmetics aisle to find something more fitting to my lengthy to-do list... or I could just get used to going everywhere fresh-faced.

Haha, right. It's not like I had many wrinkles or pimples to cover up, but the simple act of applying my daily powders and glosses gave me a special kind of courage. Knowing I looked good helped me get through the day. I'd never been a great beauty, but I liked showing others that I cared about my appearance and thus myself. It was a routine my mom had taught me while I was quite young. I still fondly remembered those middle school mornings spent applying our foundation and blush side by side in the massive bathroom mirror.

I smiled as I thought of Mom all the way back home in Michigan. Once this investigation was officially closed, I'd have to give her a call to catch up. Unfortunately, if I called any sooner, she'd see right through any attempts I made to downplay my anxiety.

And so it would have to wait.

In all the talk about Harold and the non-talk about Luna, I hadn't managed to eat breakfast, so by the time I reached the restaurant my stomach had begun to sing a mournful tale of neglect, one growl and one grumble at a time.

The BBQ Shack was something of a local legend and often boasted a long wait for anyone to be seated. I hadn't yet been, but the moment I stepped inside and smelled the sweet, tangy scents of barbecue, saliva began to pool in my mouth.

Kelley was already seated at a table toward the front and motioned for me to join her. She stood when I arrived and motioned between me and her mother, a dour-looking woman who was so thin, her cheeks appeared sunken in. "Gracie, this is my mom. Mom, Gracie."

Kelley's mother remained seated but extended her hand for a limp shake. I couldn't tell whether I disliked her or whether I simply had a bad reaction to believing she didn't like me. Whatever the case, I immediately became very uncomfortable. The only saving grace was that the noisy revelry of the other diners was enough to drown out the sounds my singing stomach.

Nobody said anything until the waitress arrived to take my drink order. Kelley and her mom had already settled in with a couple Arnold Palmers, so I ordered the same.

When it became clear that Kelley still didn't know what to say and her mother had no desire to start a conversation herself, I folded my hands in front of me and did the deed myself. "So what do you think of Elderberry Heights, Mrs....?" *Shoot,* I didn't even know Kelley's last name.

"Carmine," my friend supplied with a tight grin.

"And it's Miss, thank you very much. I never married after a certain boyfriend turned me off of love and marriage forever." She sniffed and grabbed the small mesh container that housed packets of multi-colored sugars and artificial sweeteners.

"Mom," Kelley whined, kicking her heels back against her chair with a thump that resonated through the table. "You promised you wouldn't talk about Dad anymore.

"Well, it's not my fault, your friend brought him up. Also don't call him 'Dad.' that man was never a father to you."

"I didn't... I mean, I'm sorry if—"

"No, no. Don't apologize," Kelley said gently to me, then turned her head to glare at her mother. "Stop trash-talking him. I get that what happened between you wasn't great, but the man is dead. Just let it go."

Ms. Carmine snorted and dumped two packets of Splenda into her cold drink, taking care to stir them vigorously with her straw.

Seeing as things were already tense, I decided to prod a little. "What did happen between you?"

Kelley's eyes widened and her lips puckered, but she made no move to argue. The look on her face said it all, though. I'd betrayed her in the worst possible way.

I hated that I'd hurt my new friend, but I could apologize for that later. She'd thank me once I helped to bring her father's murderer to justice—even if that murderer ended up being her own mother.

"What happened between us?" Ms. Carmine repeated, her voice pitchy and agitated. "What happened between us?"

Kelley placed a hand on her mother's shoulder and mouthed something I couldn't decode. "Same old girl loves boy, boy cheats on girl, and they lived unhappily ever after story," she told me, then raised an arm and shouted, "Waitress! I think we're ready to order."

"He didn't just cheat on me," Ms. Carmine bit out. "He did it with my roommate who also happened to be my very best friend. I had nowhere else to go, so I left town. I vowed if he ever turned up at my door again, I'd kill him with my bare hands."

"Mom!" Kelley cried, jumping to her feet. "Enough!"

Ms. Carmine silently sipped at her tea. To her credit, she was in a much better mood for the remainder of our meal after she'd gotten whatever that was off her chest.

And the whole time we ate and made small talk, I kept on wondering: Had Kelley's mom just confessed to Harold's murder?

And if so, what should I do next?

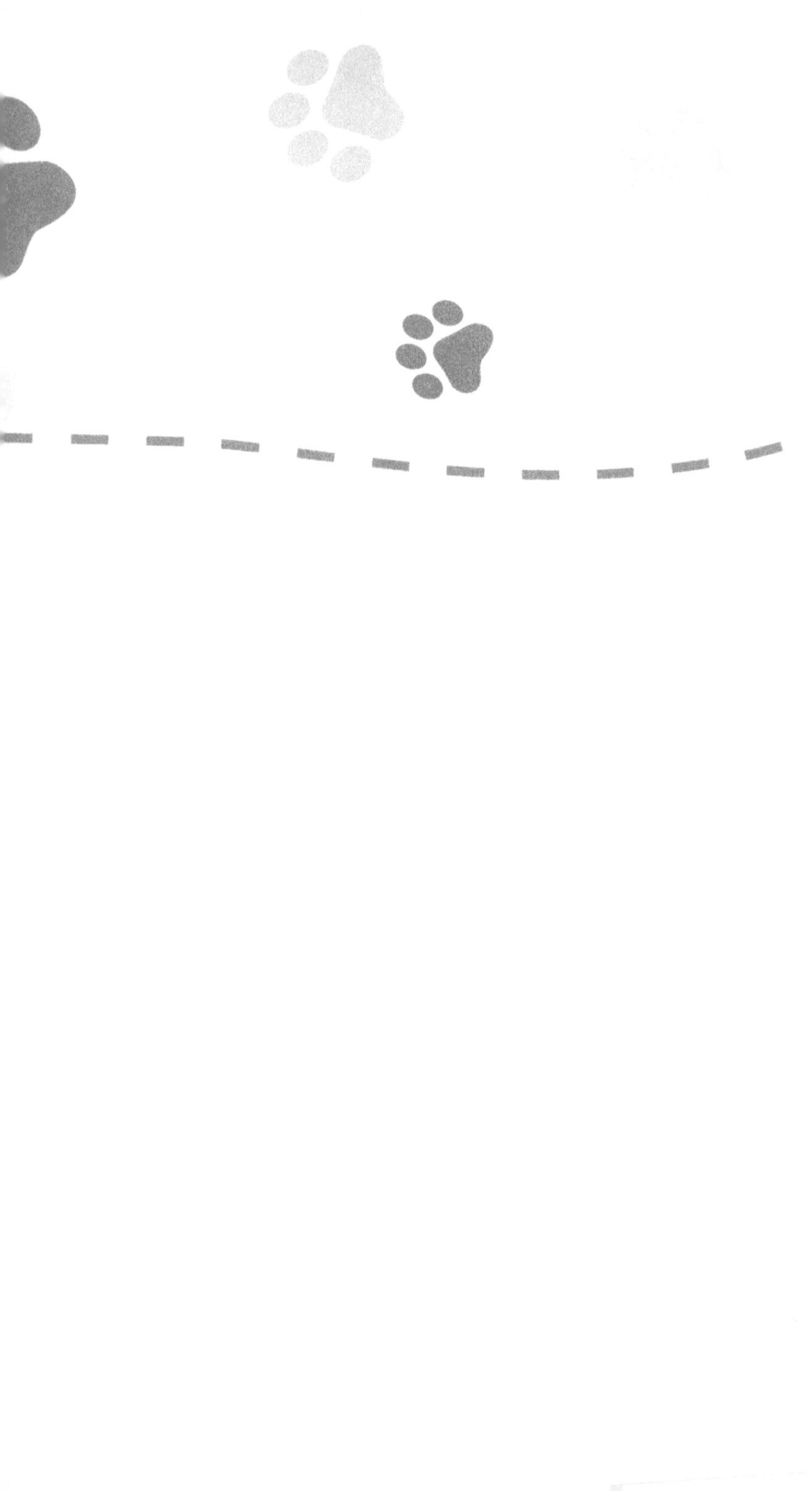

19

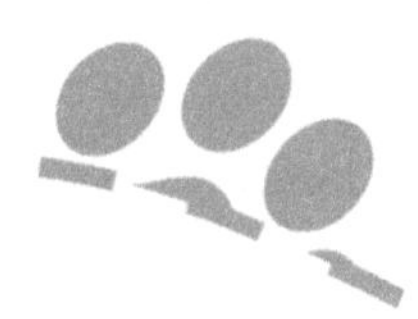

hen I returned home from my lunch outing, I found my cat waiting for me by the front door.

"Where were you?" he demanded with an angry flick of his tail.

"Something came up, and I had to help a friend," I explained as I crossed the room and flopped down on the couch.

"You smell like barbecue sauce," Merlin accused. His nose twitched unhappily.

"That help involved taking her out to lunch. But that's not what's important here." I leaned forward and steepled my fingers. "I think I know who killed Harold."

Merlin jumped up onto the sofa beside me and

allowed me to run my fingers through his thick double coat. "So you've got it all figured out, do you? Enlighten me, then."

"It was Ms. Carmine. She's the mother of one of the other baristas, Kelley. And Harold was Kelley's father. There was no love lost between them, let me tell you. Add in the fact that Harold was poisoned with gas line antifreeze and that Officer Dash is convinced someone from out of state did the deed, and the fact she all but confessed over lunch, and there you have it."

"Interesting," Merlin said from his place beside me. "One hundred percent wrong, but interesting, nonetheless."

"Wrong?" My heart sank, and I pulled my hand away. "Why do you think that? I've already thought really long and hard about this, and Ms. Carmine definitely did it."

"I don't merely *think* you're wrong. I know it." He sat up and puffed his furry chest with pride. "I just paid a visit to our old friend Harold, and I can say with absolute certainty that he was poisoned by a magical potion. Not... what was it you said? Antifreeze?" He chuckled quietly and shook his head.

"But Officer Dash said—"

"Officer Dash lied," he said flatly.

No, this didn't make sense, and I'd tell him that if he would just let me finish a sentence. "Why would a police officer lie?"

Merlin hung his head, his ears thrust back in consternation. "That's a good question. You can't exactly ask her. She'll just lie again."

"I'm going to the station," I said, shifting back toward the door. "Something's not right here."

"I'm coming with you," he insisted.

"Are we going to teleport? Because the station is on a pretty busy street. Someone will see."

Merlin jumped off the couch and then turned to face me. "You drive. I'll meet you there. First I have some business with my cauldron."

"What are you going to do? Can't we just drive together? I'd feel safer if I had you with me." I was in a sad state considering I felt that I needed my cat's company in order to stay safe.

He didn't budge despite my pleas. "I'm a cat, Gracie. Cats don't do cars. Besides, I'll already be at the station and waiting by the time you get there. I just need a few minutes to mix a truth potion. Since I'm a sky witch, I can deliver it by air. All your officer... what was it? Nash?"

"Dash," I corrected. "She's the one with the bad attitude and permanent scowl, remember?"

He grimaced then, showing off one pearly white fang. "Dash, okay. But how could I remember when I have yet to meet her?"

"She's already been here two times in less than twenty-four hours. How is it you haven't been here for any of her little visits?"

"Dunno, but don't worry about it too much. My truth potion will be a gas rather than a liquid. I only need to breathe it out and she to breathe it in for her to fall under its spell. We'll know everything within a matter of minutes."

"Great, because I am already so sick of this investigation."

Merlin shook his head. "We still need to toughen you up. You'll deal with much worse than this serving your role as my familiar."

I rolled my eyes hard. "Oh, goody. I can hardly wait."

Merlin clearly didn't appreciate my attitude, but that didn't stop me from feeling exhausted, afraid, and in a foul mood.

"Stop with the sarcasm. It's not very becoming for a familiar," he hissed.

"I'm more than just a familiar. I'm a person,

too," I reminded him, not exactly sure where this was coming from. I guess I just had things to say, questions that had gone unanswered for too long, even though it hadn't been long at all.

"Why did you choose me?" I blurted out.

Merlin turned to stare at me head on. He blinked slowly, then stopped. "I didn't choose you, Gracie. I chose your grandmother. Remember, I was already here when you showed up."

"So you wanted her but got me. Right, I'm just one big mistake," I pouted. His confession hurt far more than I'd have expected it to.

"An accident, yes. Mistake, no. I watched you for months before revealing myself. I had to make absolutely sure," he confessed softly. "I hadn't planned for it to be you, but I'm glad it is."

I chanced a smile. "Really?"

"Really. Now enough with the mushy stuff." He moved toward the door and stopped in front of the pet flap. "We need to focus on the task ahead. I want you to drive straight to the police station. No pit stops or detours. Straight there, and I'll be waiting with the truth potion ready to go. We'll go in together."

"Yes, boss," I said with a nod. Our short chat just now had given me a renewed sense of purpose.

Merlin hadn't chosen me initially, but he chose me now.

As it turned out, that mattered a lot.

With his support and encouragement, I would be okay. And thanks to the plan he'd concocted, we could scrub my name from the suspect list within mere minutes.

I was going to be okay...

In part, because I didn't really have any other options.

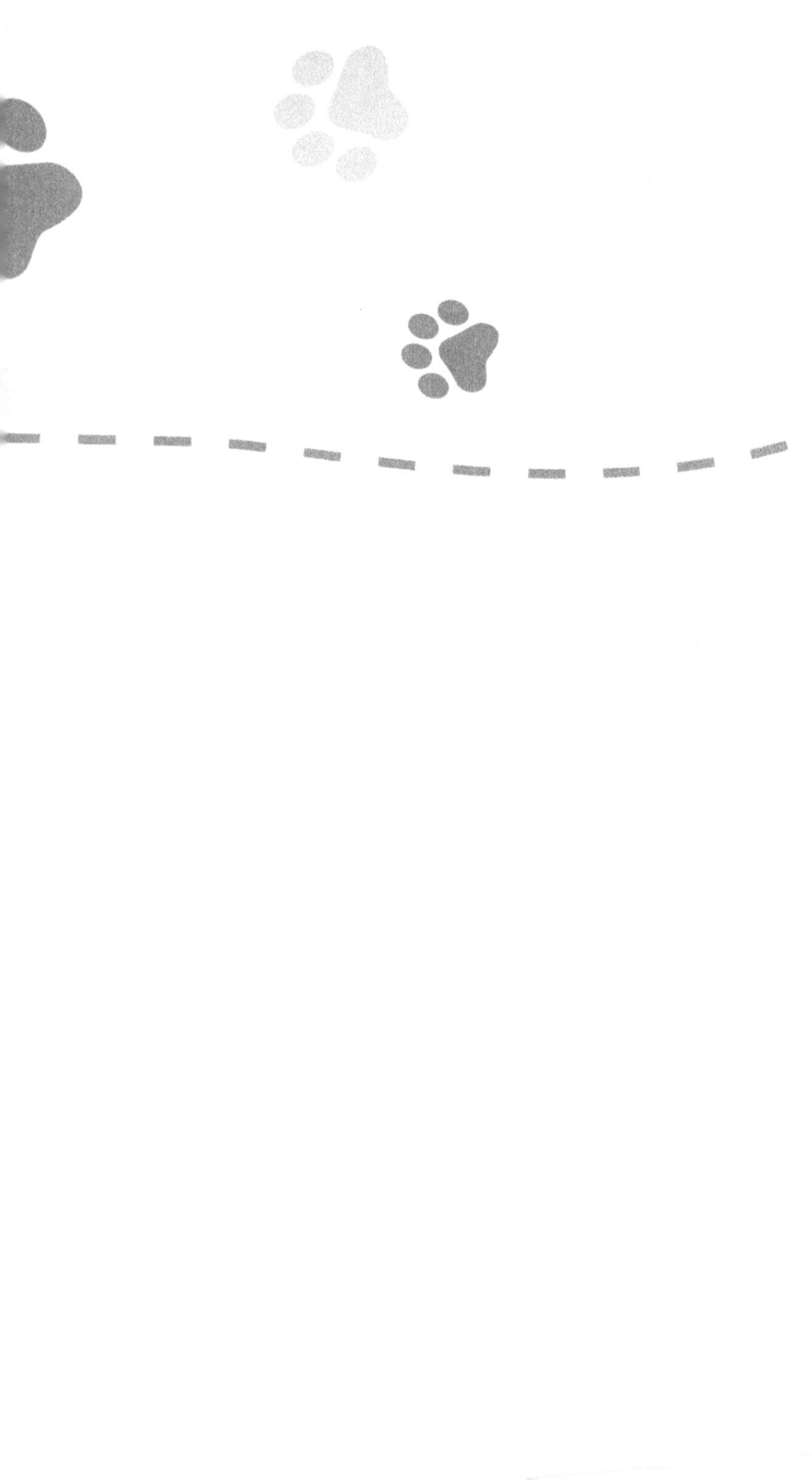

20

erlin and I both marched outside. He headed to the yard to do some work with his bird bath cauldron, and I climbed into my car and backed out of the driveway. It would take me about five minutes to reach the police station, which meant I had precious little time to sort through my latest thoughts.

According to Merlin, Officer Dash had lied to me about the poison that killed Harold. But why? The simple answer would be that the medical examiner couldn't trace the presence of magic and truly thought gas line antifreeze was to blame.

But something in my gut told me that wasn't quite right.

Had Officer Dash knowingly lied to me to see

how I responded? But if she'd intentionally lied, did that mean she knew magic was to blame? Or had she yet to hear anything conclusive from the medical team?

Once again, I wound up lost in the churning sea of my thoughts. So lost, in fact, that I forgot to pay attention to the road signs. I blew right through a stop sign at a quiet intersection that led out of my neighborhood, only realizing it once it was too late to brake.

Crud. I really needed to stop getting consumed by my thoughts and start paying better attention to traffic. I would be better after this quick trip to the police station. Maybe I'd start pulling to the side of the road when the urge to overthink became too great.

Yeah, that would make me less of a hazard to myself and others. And yet...

It seemed I'd made this vow too late, because a police cruiser pulled out after me and turned on its siren.

No, no, no!

Yes, I'd been caught and deserved to be punished for it. I'd find some way to pay the ticket. Right now, I was more worried about the delay in joining Merlin at the police station. Hopefully this routine traffic stop wouldn't add too much time to my trip. And, yeah, maybe Merlin would be mad about having to wait a few extra minutes, but it wasn't like running from the police was a viable option here, especially since I was heading straight toward their HQ, anyway.

I groaned and pulled over to the side of the road. The cruiser pulled over behind me, and I watched through my rearview mirror as a uniformed officer climbed out and slammed the car door shut.

Officer Dash, herself.

Double crud.

She motioned for me to roll down my window, and I instantly complied.

"Well, well, well," she said with a dry chuckle. "You just can't stay out of trouble. Can you, Springs?"

"I'm sorry," I murmured, hating this—hating it so very much.

"License, registration, and proof of insurance, please," she barked, all business.

I slowly reached into the glove department and grabbed the needed documents, then took my license from my purse and handed that over, too.

"I'll be right back," Officer Dash told me.

I stared straight ahead as I waited for her to run my information and issue my ticket. Time passed much more quickly than I would have imagined, because it seemed like only moments later, Officer Dash returned to the driver's side of my car.

"Out of the vehicle," she ordered with a cold, assessing gaze.

"What? Why?" I squeaked.

"Don't ask questions. Just do what I say!" she shouted.

Her sudden fit of rage frightened me so much that I stumbled out of my car as told. And though she frightened me, I hoped she'd be less frightening if I complied with orders.

"Hands against the vehicle," Officer Dash spat.

"What? No. I didn't do anything wrong!" I shouted.

Dash pushed me into the side of my car. Hard.

Pain shot through my shoulder, burning even worse as she grabbed my wrists and slapped a pair of handcuffs on them.

"I didn't do anything," I sobbed. "Please let me go."

"Stop whining and turn to face me!"

When I turned, a giant Cheshire smile filled the

policewoman's face. She was loving every moment of this.

"I don't understand," I mumbled. "Did you find new evidence?"

Instead of answering, Officer Dash place a hand on my shoulder and forced me to meet her gaze. I watched in silent horror as her eyes changed color and shape, shifting from unassuming gray to a bright and robust green.

She blinked once... Twice...

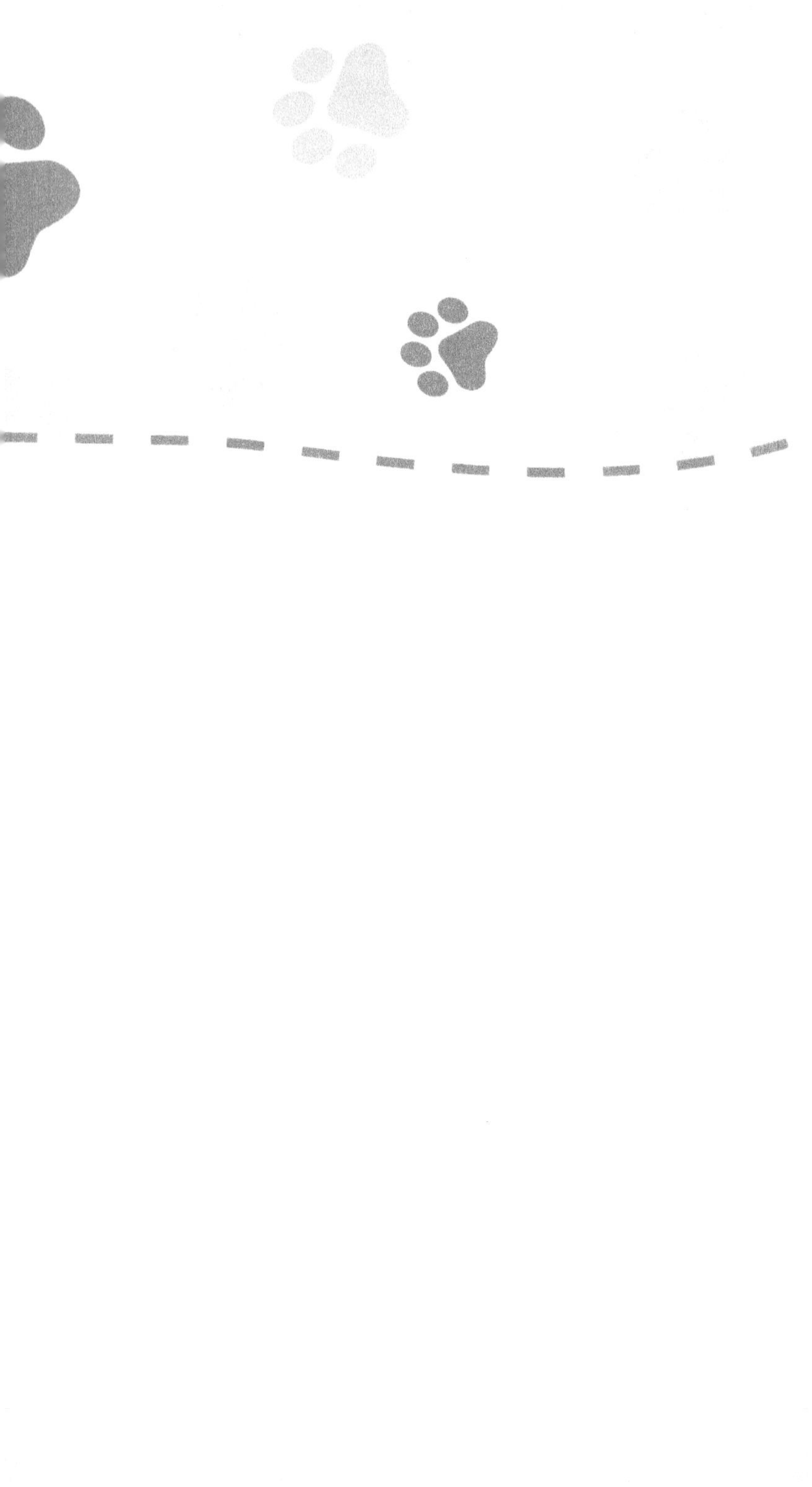

21

I crashed into the earth, unable to catch myself, thanks to my wrists being cuffed behind my back. I kicked out with my legs and twisted my torso, struggling to bring myself into a sitting position. At last I rammed into a thick tree trunk and was able to wiggle myself upward.

Once I had a moment to take in my surroundings, I recognized the small garden cottage almost instantly. We'd come to Luna's, and I was pressed against the same Magnolia tree I'd clutched onto after my very first teleportation.

The front door of the quaint brick house flew open, and Virginia ran outside in bare feet. Her toenails were painted in a shiny lavender I wouldn't have expected from her.

"Oh, goody!" she cried, racing into the yard. "Is it time at last?"

"It is." Officer Dash spoke from behind me. I twisted in an effort to see her, but the thick magnolia tree blocked her from view.

"What do you want with me?" I shouted to whoever was willing to answer.

"I've got this one," Virginia announced, sauntering forward with a soft expression that belied the vitriol of her words. "You should've been in jail by now, but your bond to that stupid cat formed too fast, which means Plan B became necessary."

"I didn't kill Harold," I told her as I struggled to slip my wrists from the handcuffs. The task seemed impossible, but that didn't mean I'd stop trying. Especially since this seemed to be shaping into a try-or-die type of situation.

"Of course you didn't," Virginia said with an almost-pleasant smile. "I did."

"You?" I asked, my voice now shaking with fear. I hadn't even considered her. Luna, yes. But her powerless familiar? Never.

Virginia simpered at me. "Don't you remember asking me to leave the coffeehouse that day? I was sitting right there. I thought for sure you'd put it together when you showed up at my house yesterday, but no. Turns out you're not that smart, after all."

"You were the customer!" I shouted as the final pieces clicked into place. No wonder Virginia had seemed so familiar. She'd been sitting in plain sight that day. Amateur sleuth or not, how had I missed something so major in my investigation?

Virginia's smile widened. I had the sudden urge to slap it right off her face, in part for Harold and in part for me. "See, Dash. She does catch on eventually."

Officer Dash didn't respond, so I took the opportunity to ask a very important question. "Are you going to kill me, too?"

Finally, Virginia's tight smile disappeared. "Unfortunately, no. You've made things quite difficult for us, I'll have you know. You were supposed to take the fall for that old miser's death so the authorities could shut you up and throw away the key before your bond with Merlin had a chance to solidify. It was our best chance of getting rid of him, but you ruined that for us."

"What?" I snapped as I scowled up at her. "Do you want me to apologize?"

"Uh! No manners." Virginia let out a few slow breaths before continuing. "Any murders that happen within the magical community are instantly traced. If I would have killed you outright, then I'd find myself locked up. But since your former coffee boss knows nothing of the magical world, his death wouldn't have registered."

"Do we really need to do the whole villain monologue thing right now?" Dash growled from somewhere I still couldn't see. "We've caught her. Now we need to dispose of her."

"So you *are* going to kill me?" I shouted with triumph. I had been right, but I wish I hadn't.

"Worse," Virginia revealed with wide, bright eyes. She enjoyed this, the villain.

"What? What's worse than death?" I asked. I had to keep her talking, to give Merlin time to find and rescue me.

Virginia played straight into the wicked stereotype and threw her head back to cackle. "You'll see soon enough, my dearie."

"But I don't understand. Why did you want me out of the way? What did I ever do to you?"

"Absolutely nothing," Virginia admitted with a sniff. "But Dash wanted Merlin out of the picture, and I was all too happy to oblige, given the history between him and my boss."

So this was because my playboy cat had broken the wrong cat's heart. *Ugh!*

"People fall in love and break up all the time," I argued. "That doesn't mean you kill them."

"Oh, I don't care about that. Although all of Luna's incessant pining for that scruffy fleabag has certainly gotten on my last nerve."

"Then what do you want?"

"Magic is volatile. Did you know that? The more of it that exists within the same area, the more likely it is to cause an unwanted reaction. When Merlin took you on as his familiar, Luna's magic had to be dampened to protect the town. I certainly see no reason why either of us should be deprived of the level of power we've grown accustomed to, so when my companion here offered a plan to dispose of you both, I eagerly agreed to do my part."

"But how does getting rid of me keep Merlin from finding a new familiar?"

She hung her head and let out a deep laugh. "You really don't know much about how this community works. Do you? Once a familiar has been initiated, it's almost impossible for a witch to obtain a new one. Not after that whole mess with the two Merlins and Arthur way back when. And without his familiar close by, *our* Merlin can't legally practice magic. The powers that be would lock him up so quick, he wouldn't even have the chance to blink away."

"Enough!" Dash shouted from behind me. "She's just trying to buy herself time in case that kitty cat of hers shows up to rescue her. I'm done dawdling. Let's finish what we started."

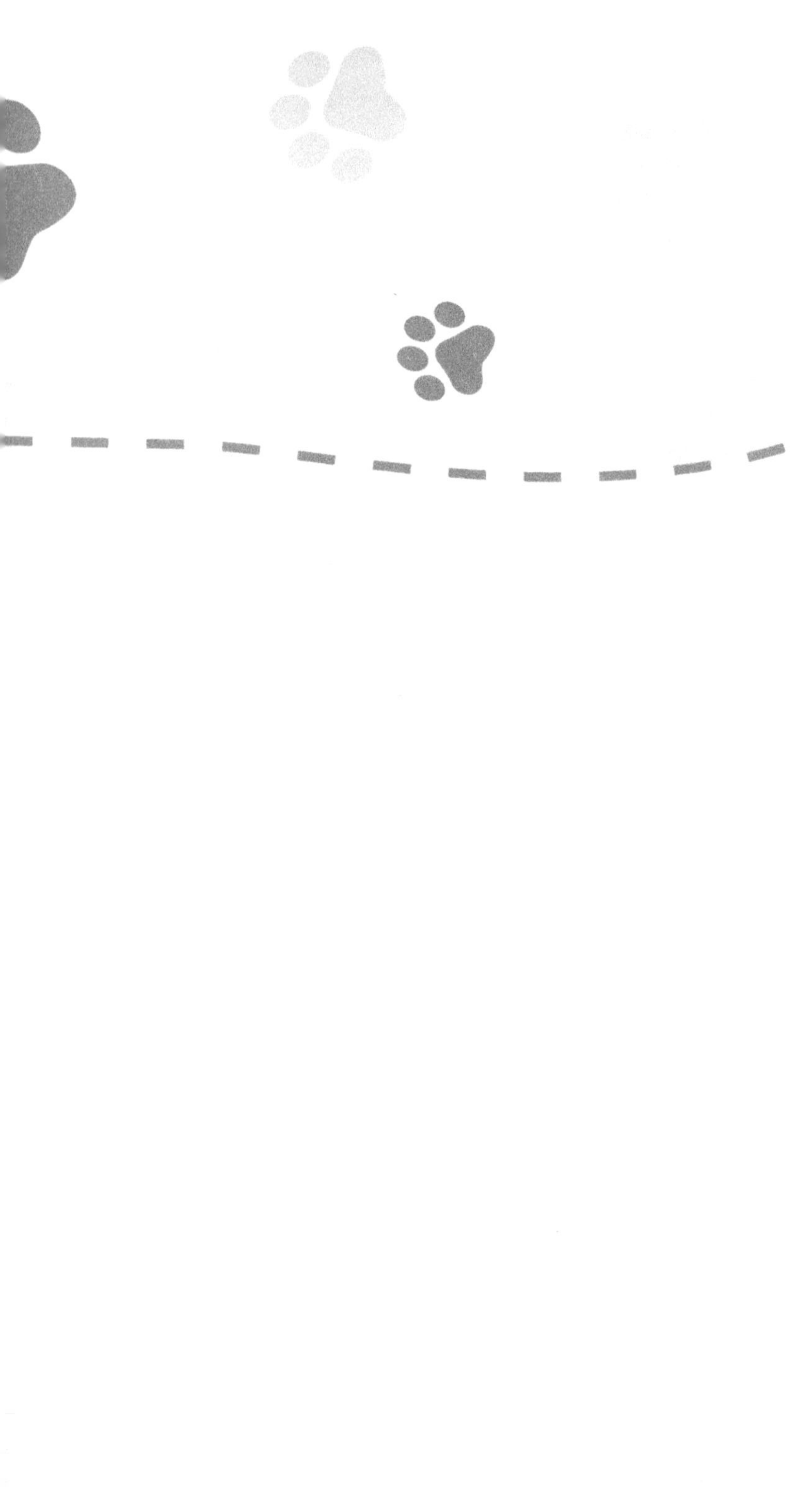

22

As soon as she vowed to "finish what we started," Officer Dash at last stepped into my line of sight. She looked the same as she always had, except the bright green eyes. Eyes like mine, like Virginia's, like anyone who'd been touched by magic.

"You're not a real cop," I spat at her.

"Oh, really. What was your first clue?" The fake officer Dash laughed at me cruelly, then raised both hands and snapped her fingers above her head.

The air around her rippled and shimmered with a slightly green hue as she transformed from the sardonic police officer into a chunky black cat with a crooked tail.

I gasped, and so did Virginia.

"You're a witch," she cried, pointing an accusing finger at her accomplice. "This whole time you told me you were a familiar, too. That you were fed up with the status quo."

The black cat smiled devilishly. "Dearest Virginia, one of those things is true. The other? Well, you played into my hand so easily, a fact which I most definitely appreciate. But now that your usefulness has expired, I no longer need you."

The cat version of Dash clicked her tongue, and Virginia's face grew into a mask of horror. Her mouth opened wide in a silent scream, and her feet shuffled hopelessly beneath her as she floated a foot from the ground.

"What did you do to her?" I demanded, struggling even harder against my bonds now. I couldn't tear my eyes away from Virginia, terrified that I would share her fate. Why wasn't she screaming? It would be easier to take if she screamed.

Dash unsheathed her claws and stared down at them, thinking. "Why do you care? She killed your boss and tried to send you to jail for it."

"We both know you were the mastermind. Virginia was only a pawn in your scheme," I shouted. We were on the edge of a large subdivision. Maybe if I screamed loud enough one of the neighbors would hear and come to my rescue.

"I bet you never even told her why you wanted Merlin out of the picture," I muttered when Dash continued to stare down at her claws without even acknowledging my previous accusation.

"Virginia had her own silly reasons for what she did. She didn't need to know mine."

"Tell me," I demanded, kicking my feet out before me to appear like more of a threat. "I deserve to know."

"You deserve nothing!" Dash hissed. "And you will get nothing except what's coming to you!"

With that, she leaped toward me. Rather than unleashing a storm of magic, she sliced a claw against my cheek. I instantly forgot the dull ache in my shoulders in favor of the sharp sting that took over. I screamed out in pain, but the movement in my facial muscles only made it hurt that much more. A drop of fresh blood rolled down my cheek and fell onto my shirt, leaving an ugly red stain.

Dash ignored my misery as she floated back to the ground and studied her blood-tipped claws, green eyes wide with wonder. "*Huh.* Well, that explains a few things."

"What things? What's going on? Why are you

doing this to me?" I cowered against the tree, which seemed to please the evil black cat.

She paced back and forth for a moment before turning toward me once again. "My blabbermouth assistant already told you more than you need to know, but I'll let you in on one last little piece of knowledge."

Dash looked back over her shoulder at Virginia, who was still trapped in soundless torment. "Look at her. She's currently living her worst nightmare."

And I knew from the frozen mask of terror on Virginia's face that Dash was being truthful with me now.

I shuddered, hating that the truth was scarier than a lie. Why else would Dash have revealed this to me? "What is it?" I sputtered, groping for words, willing to do anything to keep the conversation going. "Spiders? Clowns? Great White Sharks?"

Dash smiled. "That's the beauty of illusion magic. I don't need to know. The magic finds the fears, the desires, finds whatever I need and latches right onto it. Virginia was a fool, but it was even easier to convince her to fall in line when my magic probed her heart and found what I needed."

"You're an illusion witch?" I gasped. I didn't

know exactly what that meant, but it certainly sounded scary.

Dash smiled at me again. "The very best that ever lived."

"I know why Virginia wanted to get rid of Merlin, but why you?" Strangely, I was beginning to wish that Dash would turn back into the ornery policewoman. This new feline version was much, much worse.

She shook her head. *"Ah, ah, ah!* I have no need to reveal my plot to the likes of you. I only told you about Virginia so you'd know what was about to happen to you and fear it all the more."

I met her eye, unwilling to cower in fear any longer. "You'll never get away with—"

But Dash cut me off by loudly clicking her tongue twice. As soon as she did, the whole world melted away, leaving me trapped in a sea of endless black.

Noooooooo!

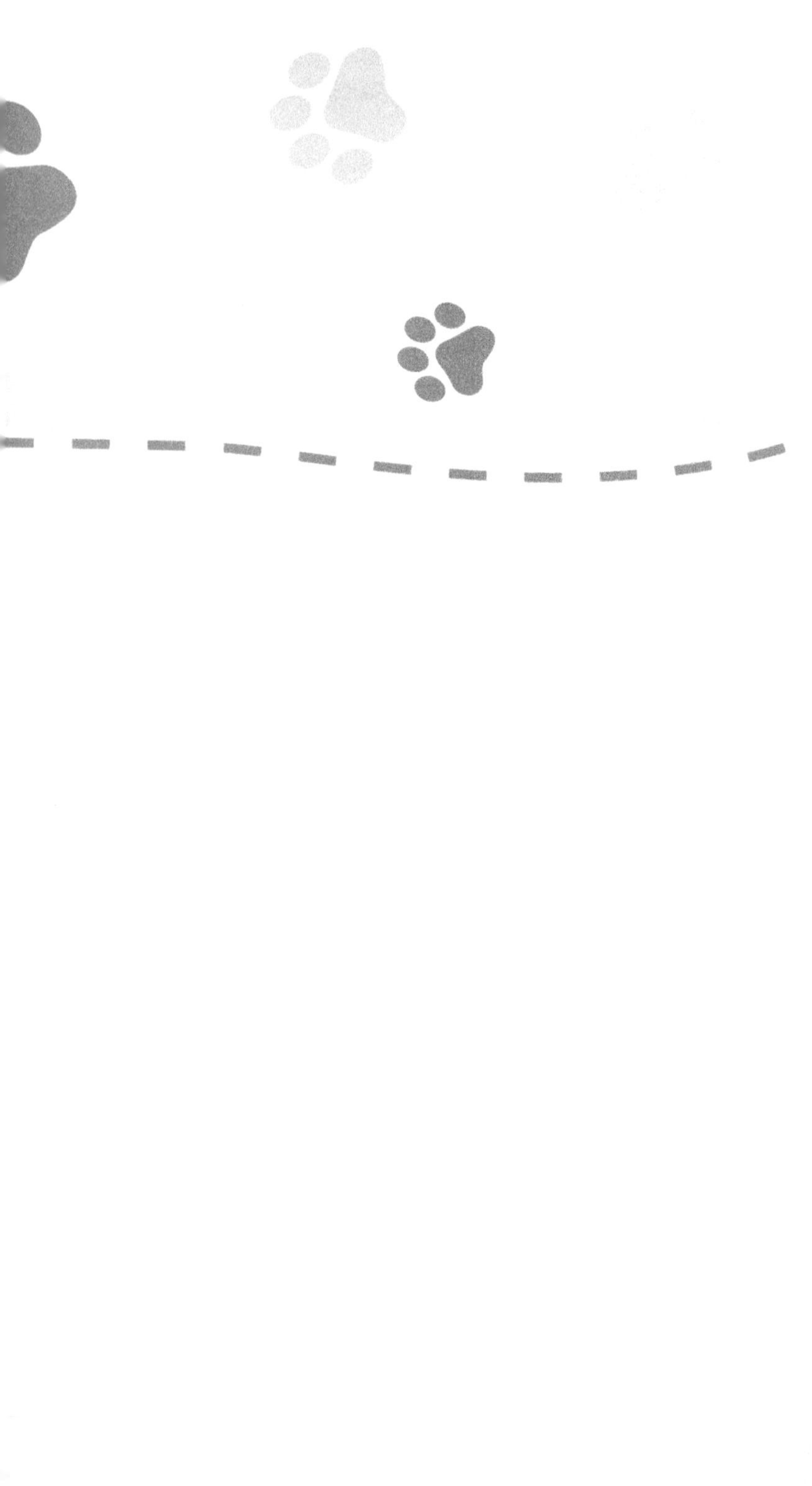

23

"Hello?" I cried into the echoing void, but no one answered. Unnerved, I stumbled forward, unable to feel the ground over which my feet moved. I couldn't feel anything, not even the cool metal which had previously bound my wrists.

A pinprick of light appeared on the horizon, and I rushed toward it, desperate to get out of this dark place. I still couldn't bring my hands forward despite not being able to feel the cuffs on my skin, which resulted in my waddling more than jogging toward my destination.

As I moved closer, the tiny light pulsed and expanded, and out stepped Merlin in all his Maine

Coon glory. Instead of normal shining green, his eyes were deep black, lifeless, soulless.

"I didn't choose you. I got stuck with you," he sneered, addressing my secret fear head-on.

"No, no. It's not true," I said, recalling our earlier conversation. I hadn't been his initial choice, but he was very happy that we'd ended up together.

"You're lying," I bit out.

And with that, the false Merlin burst into a puff of smoke and floated off into the darkness.

"You were an illusion," I told myself. "Just an illusion."

I'd called the imposter cat on his lie and he'd left me alone. I just had to remember to find the truth. Hopefully it would set me free from this awful place.

Another pale flicker of illumination appeared to the distant right, so I stepped toward it, bracing myself for what I might find there.

A tall man's silhouette appeared. I couldn't make out his features but recognized him as soon as he spoke. *Harold.*

"You may not have killed me, but it's your fault I'm dead," he told me with great anger.

What could I say to that? I couldn't deny the part I'd played. This accusation was perfectly true.

Harold kept going, feeding my guilt, making it grow bigger and bigger.

"I always knew you were a worthless employee, but I kept you on out of the kindness of my heart. And how did you repay me? Ha!"

"I'm sorry," I mumbled as tears began to form in the corners of my eyes, making my vision blurry. "I'm really, really sorry."

"A little too late for that," he scoffed. "And what happens if you get yourself out of this alive? Will you kill your next boss, too?"

"I—" My voice broke. "I didn't mean to. I'm so, so sorry."

"I have no one to mourn me, and it's your fault," he raged.

"No," I whispered, lifting my head high. "Your daughter Kelley misses you very much. All she ever wanted was the chance to know you. And she's still trying to find out who you were, even though you're gone, even though her mother doesn't want her to. And I'm trying to help. I shared stories with her. I helped her stand up to her mother..."

That's when it hit me.

"I never liked you very much," I continued, using this opportunity to get it all off my chest. "But I didn't want you to die. And it's not my fault you did. Yes, they were trying to frame me, but I didn't choose this magical world. It chose me. Even though I'm very sorry for what happened to you, Harold, it wasn't my fault."

Poof! His silhouette turned into a dark cloud of dust and blew away into the abyss.

"I'm done lying to myself!" I screamed into the encroaching darkness. "You may have trapped me in an illusion, but I know my own heart! I know my own mind!"

Officer Dash appeared as a semi-transparent hologram before me. Not the new cat form, but in her familiar cop garb. "You think you can outsmart my illusion?"

"I know I can," I shouted, wishing I could shake a fist at her.

She laughed softly at first, then more and more breathlessly. Soon Officer Dash was wheezing for breath. "You stupid girl. This isn't some family-friendly film where the princess just needs to believe in herself to defeat her much more qualified opponent. You're not a princess. You have no power, and you will not win."

"Yes, I will!" I shouted back at the hologram, but she only laughed harder.

"Fine. Do things the hard way. See if I care.

Eventually you'll figure out it's hopeless." And with that, Officer Dash disappeared, leaving me in absolute darkness.

I staggered forward, unwilling to give up. I'd defeated the first two illusions. I could defeat more. I could escape this place.

And though I wandered for ages, no more lights appeared, and soon I grew tired searching for them...

Was this really how it ended?

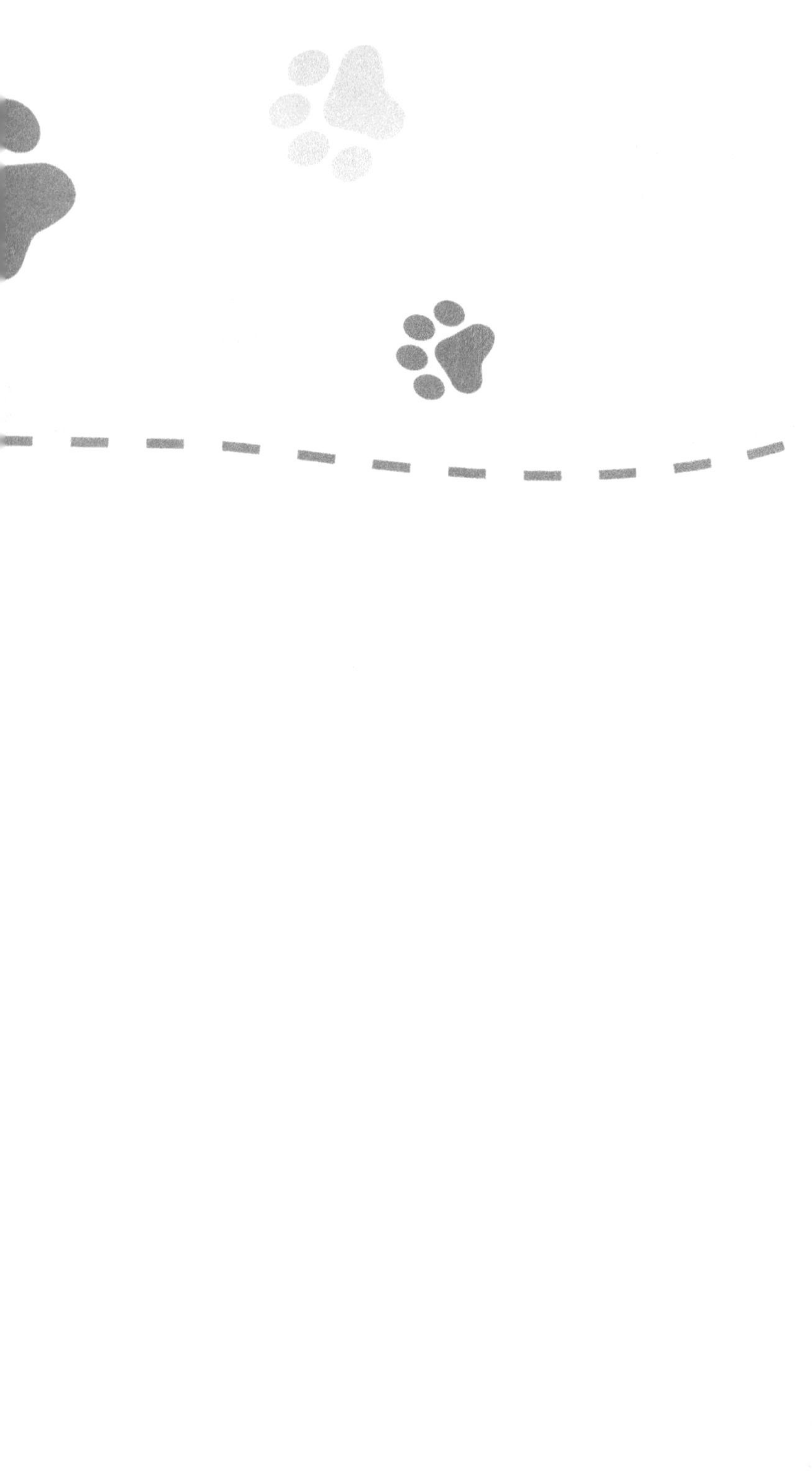

24

Even time was an illusion within that mental prison of mind. It ticked on and on leading nowhere. I would lose my mind here, if I hadn't already. I couldn't do any good for Merlin from in here, either, which meant soon he would find himself overtaken by the sinister Dash.

I didn't know why the dark witch had focused her attentions on us, but I knew now that we couldn't win. She was simply too powerful.

Battered but not yet fully defeated, I closed my eyes and tried to create my own series of mental pictures to break the monotony of the void. My mom's smile as we applied makeup side by side in that old mirror, Grandma Grace teaching me how to waltz in preparation for my first middle school dance, even Merlin speaking to me for the first time and opening my eyes to a beautiful and dangerous new world.

"Show me the truth," he said in my memory, then opened his mouth and let out a shimmering huff of magic. The darkness folded in on itself, revealing green grass, blue sky, and bright sun.

No, this wasn't a memory. It was really happening now.

"I knew that truth serum was worth the extra few minutes it took to prepare," my cat told me as he brushed his soft fur against my wrists, freeing me from the cuffs.

"What's going on?" Virginia cried as she awoke from her illusion and staggered toward us.

"Not so fast!" Merlin commanded, then kicked his hind legs into the earth and sent a pair of small cyclones spinning toward Virginia. When they reached her, they braided around her torso, trapping her within the high-speed winds.

I'd never seen such a powerful display of magic from my cat before, and now that I had, I felt very glad he was on my side.

"How did you find me?" I asked, bringing my arms in front of me to ease the ache in my shoulders. Now that I'd escaped the illusion, everything hurt again.

"Easy," Merlin revealed, kicking up another pair of twisters and dispatching them toward Dash. "I followed our familiar bond. That thing is like a beacon."

I watched as the black cat deftly dodged the windstorm, darting wildly to the side.

"If you'll excuse me for a moment, please," my cat said, shifting onto his hind legs, then slamming back down and pounding the ground before him.

A flurry of sharp icicles shot down from the sky and formed a cage around Dash, much like the one made of flowers and thorns that Luna had crafted to contain Merlin.

"You'll never defeat me," Dash hissed as she rammed her body into the icy prison bars.

"Big words for somebody who's trapped in a cage," my cat quipped. "Why have you kidnapped my familiar? And what is this other one doing here?"

Dash's hackles rose. "I don't owe you—"

"Speak the truth," Merlin said, breathing out what was left the shimmering potion fog. Whoa, my cat was a witch and a magic-breathing dragon. I'd have to remember to reflect on just how cool that was later. You know, after we got out of this alive.

The black cat strained in an effort to remain quiet, but one by one the words came out. "The... Only... One... Who... Can... Stop... Me... From... Fulfilling... My... Destiny." She emphasized this with a long and angry hiss.

Merlin traipsed over to the cage and sat just out of Dash's reach. "Oh, so this is some funny prophecy business? Strange, I thought those were outlawed."

"Not prophecy. *Lineage.*"

As Dash choked and gasped for air, Merlin casually tilted his head to the side. "What does lineage have to do with anything?"

"My... Ancest—" Dash gasped and fell on her side, letting out a long pitchy yowl. "My secret dies with the two of you!" she shouted, no longer under his spell.

"Well, that's unfortunate," Merlin said as he stalked the perimeter of the ice cage. "Because we don't feel like dying today. Do we, Gracie?"

I shook my head and mumbled, "No."

Dash clicked from inside the cage and shifted into a tiny insect, flying easily between the bars.

She transformed back into the black cat mid-flight and fell to the earth with an unsettling thud.

"Neat trick," Merlin said, raising his back and puffing out his tail like a cat on Halloween. "Wait until you see what I can do with a little bit of static electricity."

The sky darkened, and somewhere in the distance thunder boomed. I hoped the tree would shelter from me from the terrible storm that would soon be coming. Or that my cat at least had enough control to avoid hitting me with it.

"No! Merlin, stop!" a husky female voice shouted. A blur of white rushed onto the scene and thrust herself between the warring witches. *Luna!*

Virginia's missing witch had arrived, and I doubted she'd be on our side. Merlin had put up a good fight against Dash, but there was no way he'd be able to win against two more experienced witches.

I silently whispered a prayer for the both of us as I watched helplessly from the shadows of the large tree branches. I hoped I'd already stored enough magic for Merlin to be useful, because I had nothing else to offer in this fight.

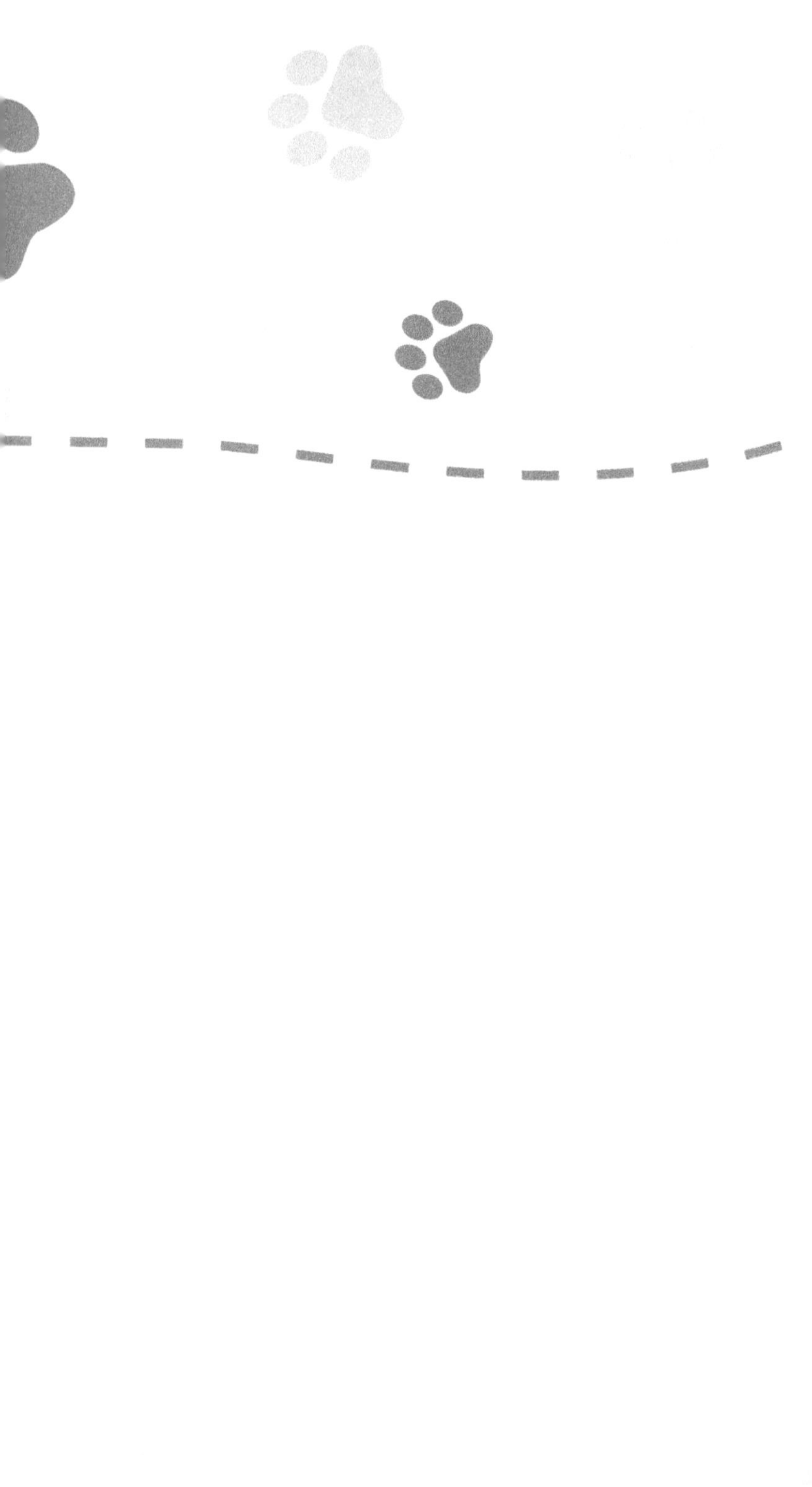

25

"I told you to stay away from my property!" Luna shouted at both me and Merlin, sweeping her searing gaze over each of us. "Now release my familiar at once!"

Merlin stared straight ahead with wide eyes, instantly complying with the garden witch's command.

"No, Merlin. Don't!" I shouted, trying to snap him out of whatever spell he was under.

"But I have to listen to Luna," he told me with a blank expression.

Uh-oh, the spell she'd forced me to give to him the other day! It had now come into effect. I remembered how helpless I'd felt as I struggled against the directive to pour the potion into his water dish, as I attempted to warn him the next morning.

I hadn't been able to stop myself from doing as it commanded, and now it seemed that Merlin couldn't, either.

Ugh. We were so dead.

Luna ran to Virginia and did a quick check for injuries. "What's going on?" she demanded of her familiar.

"I don't know," the stylish old woman sobbed.

"Lies!" Dash screamed, appearing completely unhinged as her eyes bulged from her head. She glanced straight up into the sky, then did that clicking thing that signaled a coming spell. A mirage took shape before us.

In the shaky, shimmering image, Virginia sat speaking with Officer Dash as they made the plan to kill off Harold and place the blame on me.

"But what of your witch?" Dash had asked Virginia.

"She can die, too, for all I care," Virginia seethed in the mirage.

I couldn't see Luna through the mirage, but I could hear her ask, "You would betray me?"

"She already has," Dash announced, clicking her tongue to take the image away. Whether she'd shown us an illusion or a memory, I couldn't say. Either was equally probable—and equally devastating.

Luna swished her tail and let out a keening wail. The massive magnolia tree behind me rose up from the earth.

Virginia tried to run, but the tree used one of its limbs to lift her high into the air and hold her captive.

"Why?" Luna cried, visibly straining from the effort of commanding the gigantic tree.

"You left me no choice," Virginia bit out. "Magic used to mean something to you, but lately you've been such a lovesick fool that you've paid no attention to what's really important. With his new familiar imprisoned, Merlin wouldn't have been able to practice magic anymore, and you'd have to stop pining for him and shift your focus back to growing our power."

Luna lowered her eyes, and the tree threw Virginia high into the air, then caught her again with its branches just before she crashed into the ground.

The wretched woman screamed the entire time both up and down.

Luna's whole body shook and trembled, but she

showed no signs of relenting. "There is no *our* power. It's mine. It's always been mine. You were but a servant."

"I think of you as much more than a servant," Merlin assured me as we both watched, dumb-founded.

"You don't deserve the magic you were blessed with," Virginia shouted down at her witch.

Luna cocked her head to the side, straining under the weight of her magic. "Is that so?" she asked, then nodded back toward the massive hole from which the tree had emerged.

We all watched as the tree walked on its roots and then climbed back into the earth and grew still. Once it had settled in, Luna shook off her fatigue and broke into a run.

Virginia scampered down, and the moment she touched ground, Luna jumped onto her shoulders, claws fully extended.

"Ouch!" Virginia cried, but none of us had any sympathy for her.

"You think me undeserving of my magic?" Luna asked, but didn't wait for an answer to her question. "Have it your way! I hereby renounce my power and sever the bond between us."

The ground trembled, and Virginia collapsed to her knees.

Luna jumped clear just before impact.

"What's happening?" Virginia cried as her image blinked and blurred and a cloud of shimmering green rose up from each of their bodies, creating a heavy fog that was difficult to see through.

"I am no longer a witch, and you are no longer my familiar. The magic is free!" Luna declared.

"Noooooooo!" Virginia cried, chasing after the departing fog and grasping greedily as if she could catch and hold onto the air. I couldn't see her very clearly through the magical fog. Instead, I watched the air as it shifted and moved around her.

And if I couldn't see, I doubted Virginia could, either.

Little by little, the fog condensed into itself, forming a thick, undulating wave.

Virginia remained fixated on the chase, swept away in the wave, so focused on her desperate grasp for power that she didn't consider where the expelled magic was now heading.

I watched in shocked horror as she slammed into the well that had served as Luna's cauldron and flipped over the edge, unable to catch herself before disappearing into the dark hole with the rest of the wave—returning to its source of power.

A moment later the magic had gone, and a loud crunch rose into the air.

"Well, she's dead," Merlin said beside me with not a trace of regret.

That was when I started to cry, useless non-magic entity that I was. Even though Virginia had tried to frame me for murder and send me to jail, she'd still been a living, breathing person.

Now she wasn't doing either of those things.

And with Luna and Dash still here and ready to fight, I could very well be next.

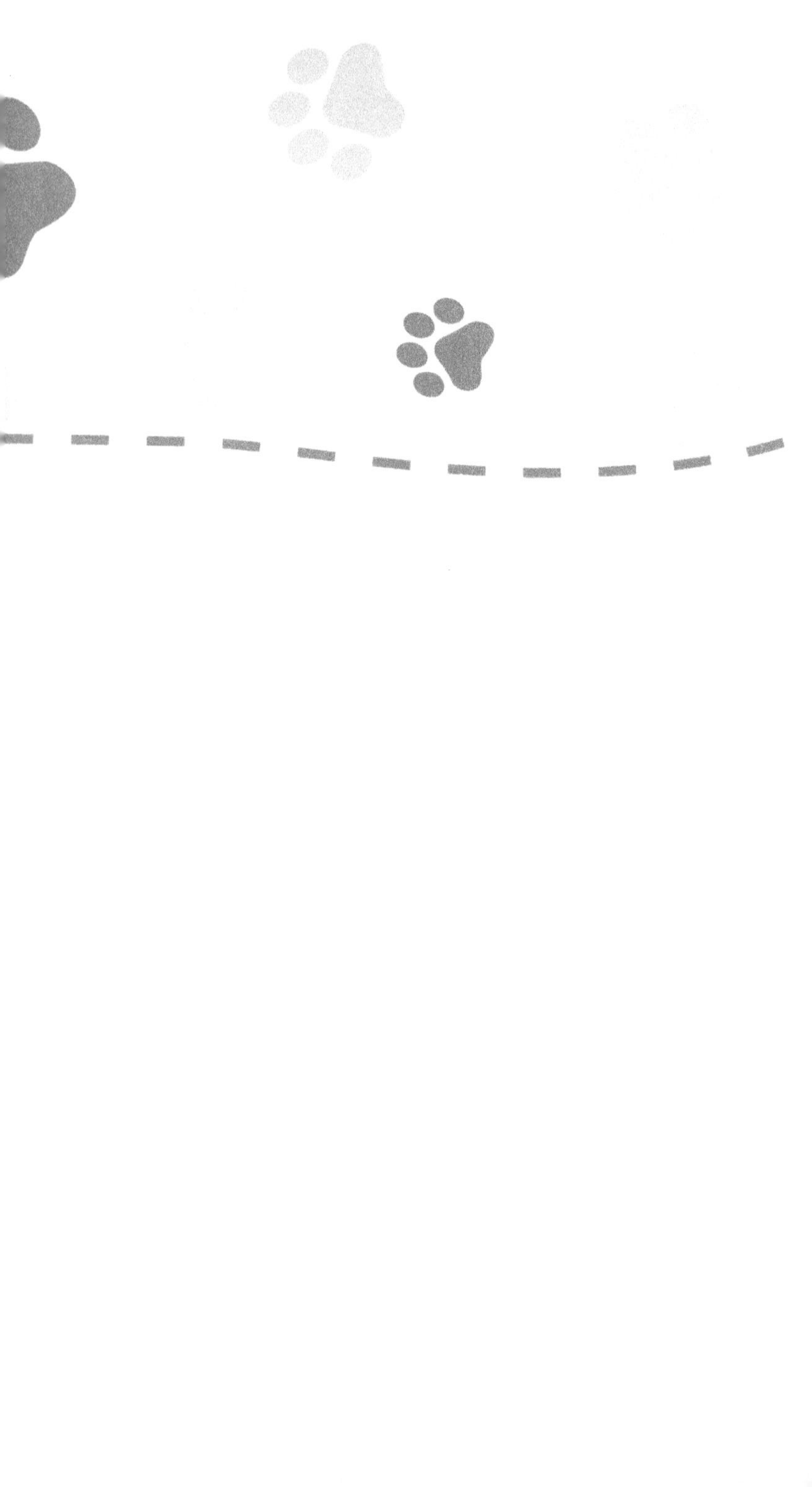

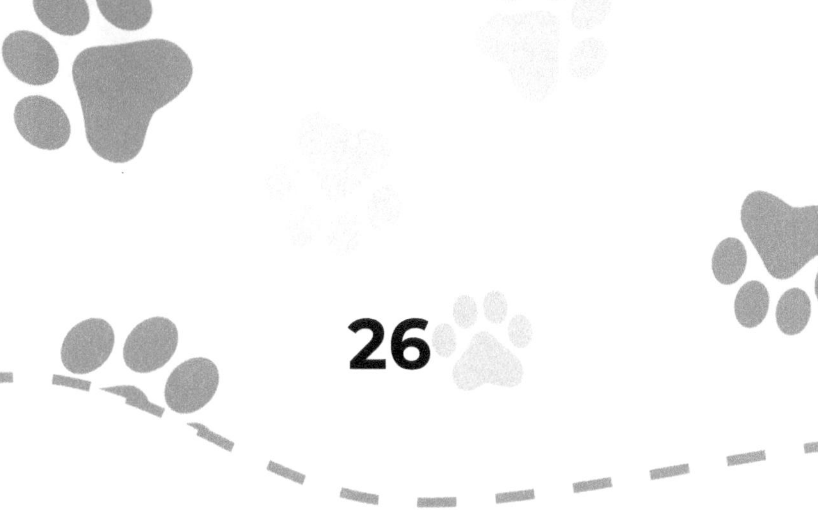

26

Luna let out a keening wail and ran to the well after her lost familiar.

"I didn't mean to kill her, only to stop her!" she cried. "Her brush with power had driven her mad. I should have been more careful before taking her on. This is all my fault."

"It's not your fault," I said, remembering my conversation with the fake Harold in Dash's illusion. Even though I'd played a part in his death, it hadn't been my fault.

The same was true for Luna now. Virginia had made her own choices. She'd betrayed her witch. She'd chased blindly after the fleeing magic, which resulted in her fatal tumble down the well.

Funny how I'd considered Luna an enemy when

she was just as hurt by today's events as both me and Merlin. I actually ached for her now as I regarded the lanky white cat, whose formerly green eyes had already begun to fade to a pale almost sickly blue.

That reminded me—she'd given up her magic. She couldn't hurt us now. She couldn't hurt us ever again.

"Where's the other one?" Merlin shouted from beside me, already kicking up his back feet in case he had to summon a twister and resume the fight.

I glanced to Merlin and then to the larger garden. Luna sat sobbing at the well, but the far more deadly Dash was nowhere to be seen.

"No! She got away," I ground out. It seemed our true nemesis had used the distraction of the magical fog to slip away undetected. Which made me wonder, had that thick cover come from the severed bond or had Dash cast the illusion herself?

"A coward!" Merlin spit at the ground, then curled his lip in disgust.

"No, she was anything but." I shook my head, wishing my cat's assertion was true but knowing better than to hope. "Both plans A and B failed, so she retreated. She'll be back with a new plan and even harder for us to defeat the next time."

"Merlin, I'm so sorry," Luna mewed from her place on the lip of the old stone well.

When it became clear that she wouldn't leave her vigil there, Merlin and I stalked over to join her.

Luna fixed her gaze on Merlin, her eyes dull and sorrowful. "My familiar tried to destroy you. I thought I was helping when I cut our magical ties, but I just created an excuse for the other one to sneak away."

While I felt bad for Luna over Virginia's death, I still couldn't let her off the hook completely. She'd had a part in this, too.

"You mixed a potion," I accused, finally able to utter the words I'd failed to speak so many times.

Now that Luna's magic was gone, it seemed the spells she'd previously cast no longer worked, either. "You forced me to give it to Merlin and made it so that I couldn't warn him."

Luna's eyes grew wide as Merlin reared up and arched his back. "Luna! Is this true?" he demanded.

The white cat hung her head in silent shame.

"It's true!" I cried, wringing my hands. "She kidnapped me and used hair from both of us to mix the potion. I wanted to tell you, Merlin. I tried so hard."

"Gracie, it's okay. I understand why you

couldn't resist the spell. You're still very new, but we'll work on building your defenses so that others have a harder time casting on you in the future. It will be okay." Merlin sounded almost fatherly in that moment. He may have been disappointed in how things had gone down, but it didn't make him love me any less.

The others were right. Our bond was strong. Not just magically, but emotionally, too.

Merlin's tender tone vanished when he turned to address the other cat. "Why, Luna? You said you had no part in the plot to imprison my familiar before our bond could fully actualize, and yet you did this?"

She let out a shuddering sigh.

"Speak!" Merlin barked, a strange sound coming from a cat, indeed.

Luna gasped and hopped down from the edge of the well and pressed her side against it. She looked to Merlin, then cast her gaze aside as if she'd been burned.

"Speak!" Merlin yelled even louder.

The lanky white cat turned her pale eyes to me. "I didn't want to hurt either of you. It was a..." She continued speaking, but her words became so soft and mumbled that I couldn't make them out.

"A what?" I prompted, leaning closer in an effort to better hear.

"A love spell. A potion to make Merlin fall back in love with me!" Luna's voice grew louder and stronger with each word.

I turned to look at Merlin, and he stood with eyes wide and unblinking, his mouth hanging slightly open.

"I love you, Merlin," she continued, stepping forward and coming to stand less than an inch from her flabbergasted ex. "I always have. I tried so hard to hate you once we took our familiars. I knew the laws of our society. And yet... Forgetting you was the one spell I couldn't cast."

She paused as they locked gazes, then took a small tentative step forward.

"Now I've given up my magic in the hope that we can be together. I will protect you all my days with or without magic to aid me. I will love you forever and always, no matter what. Will you love me, too?"

I held my breath as we both waited for Merlin's response... Honestly, I didn't know what to expect next.

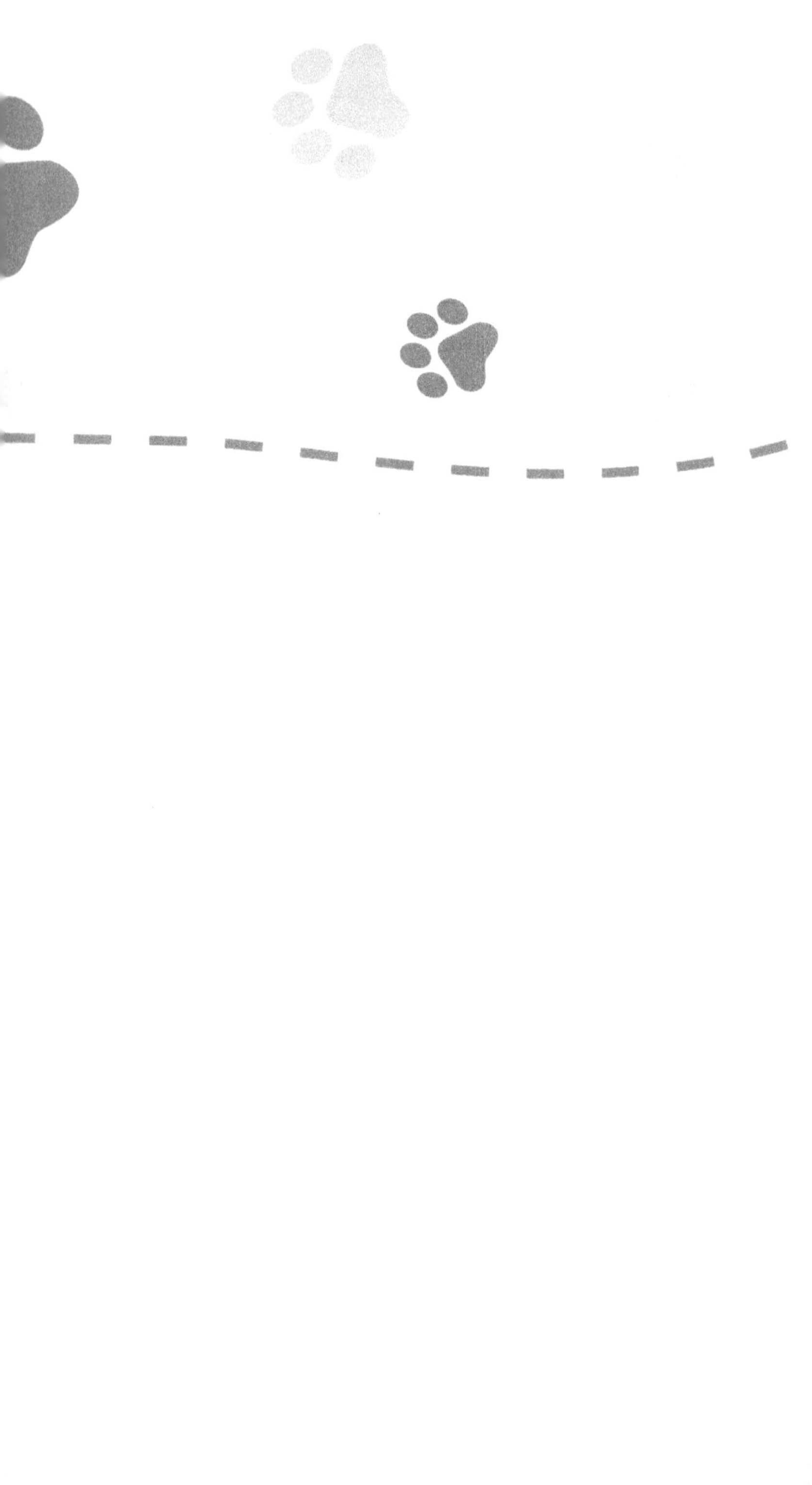

27

The battle-worn Maine Coon took one step back, then another.

Luna had just poured her heart out to him, and yet he seemed to be in search of an escape route. I loved my cat, yet a part of me vowed I would kill him if he really was planning on breaking her heart a second time.

Yes, Luna had kidnapped me, but now that I knew why, it was actually kind of sweet. Add in the fact she had given up her magic on the slight chance he'd reciprocate her love, and these cats were the stuff of classic love stories. Provided Luna's affection wasn't unrequited.

C'mon, Merlin! Tell her you love her, you big fluffy jerk!

Merlin took another step back, then turned to face the opposite direction.

And he ran.

He ran faster than I'd ever seen him run before. He moved quick and low to the ground, then zig-zagged and sprinted in the other direction.

"REOWEOEOEOW!" he cried, a cat possessed. His tail had grown puffy. He panted heavily. But still he ran and mewed and ran some more.

"I'm sorry about him," I told Luna as we both watched the spectacle.

"What's to be sorry about? He loves me back! He loves me so much that he's got the zoomies!" Luna watched Merlin's celebration with the special wonder of a woman very much in love.

I broke out laughing, such was my relief and joy. "Is that what he's doing? The zoomies?"

Merlin slowed to a trot and made his way back to us. Ignoring me, he kept his eyes glued to Luna as he approached, then closed in tight and rubbed his face against hers.

Both cats purred loudly as they continued to lick and rub against each other. The whole scene made me a bit uncomfortable, to be honest. It also made me wonder if the three of us might have a litter of witchy kittens in our near future.

When at last they came up for air, Merlin moaned, "Oh, Luna. You didn't have to cast a spell on me. I never stopped loving you. Not for one moment."

I cleared my throat, knowing that if I didn't speak now, I'd quickly be subjected to another PDA session from these two. "Um, guys. I'm really happy for you and all, but we still have some problems that need to be addressed."

"All business, this one," Luna quipped. "It seems you chose your familiar much better than I did." She glanced briefly toward the well and sighed.

Merlin moved to Luna's side, pressing his body up against hers. Although she was a tall and lanky cat, Merlin's mass of brown striped fur made him appear much larger. In fact, half of Luna's body seemed to disappear into his magical fluffiness.

Both cats watched me with rapt attention, which I guess was my permission to speak freely.

So I let it out. "Harold was still murdered, and I'm still a suspect, I think."

"You think?" Merlin asked.

"Well, Officer Dash was the one inspecting things, and apparently she wasn't a real cop. That's the part I'm not sure about." I bit my lip as I waited to hear his theory on all of this.

"The illusion witch?" Luna asked, and I nodded. I guess I could take answers from whichever cat wanted to give them.

"She won't be sticking around here where she's so easy to find," Luna assured me. "Besides, your bond with Merlin is now unbreakable. He'll be able to find and rescue you from anywhere."

"So the investigation is dead in the water?"

"The investigation was never truly alive. Dash fabricated the whole thing from the start," Merlin concluded with a smug grin.

But I still felt uneasy. "How do you know?"

"Because I saw the body, remember? I could tell he'd been murdered by magic, but to the common human observer, it would seem as though Harold passed of a severe and sudden heart attack."

I shook my head, wanting to trust him on this but also needing to be sure. "I don't understand. How did Dash expect me to take the fall for this, if everything looked normal?"

"We can't know her exact motivations, but as an illusion witch, she had many options available to her," Luna explained as Merlin purred at her side. "She could have posed as a jailer, fabricated reports, made you think you were being arrested by humans but then taken you to some kind of magical holding cell. The good news is she won't try the same thing twice, so for now you can stop worrying about her."

I sighed. "How can I stop worrying, knowing that she'll almost certainly be back?"

"That's a problem for another day," Luna told me. "Right now, bask in the moment. Live your love."

Oh, brother. I rolled my eyes hard, but neither of the two lovebirds seemed to notice or mind.

Still, I felt awful. "Fine, fine, so I'm off the hook for now, but an innocent man still died."

"That is unfortunate, but it's not like we can make it up to him," Merlin told me.

"To him, no. But there is someone else. And I have an idea..."

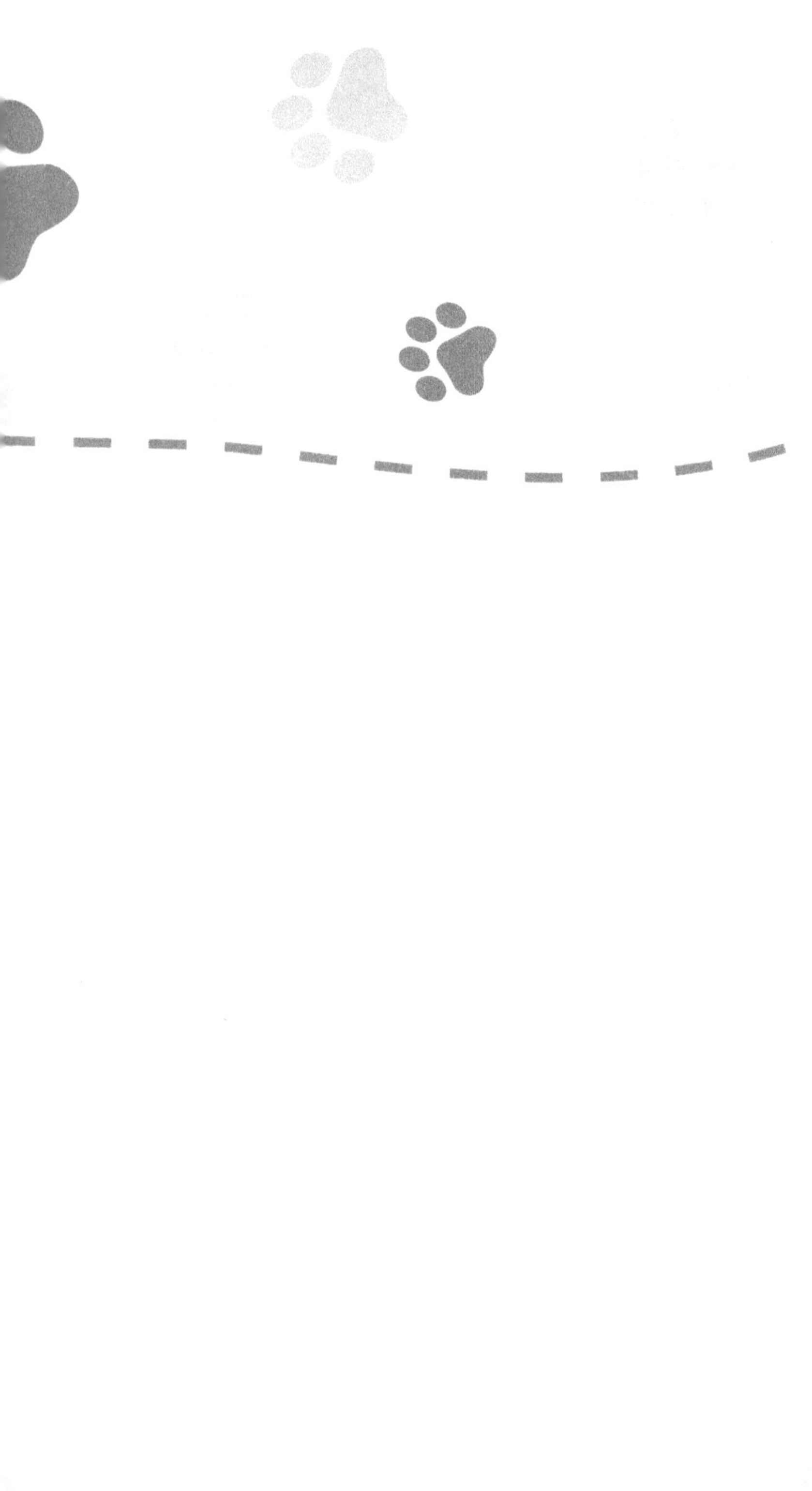

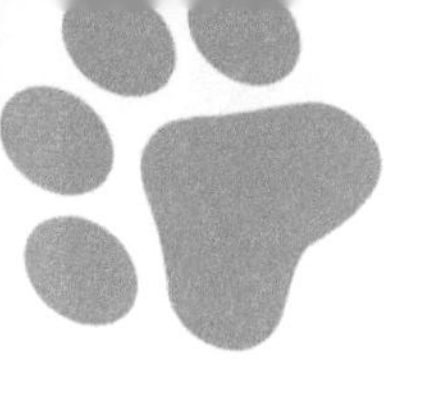

28

After our big confrontation came to its official close, Merlin teleported the three of us home.

Eventually I'd need to find my way back to my car, providing it hadn't been towed in my absence. But for now, I just needed to pop a couple painkillers and take some time to veg out on my couch.

I changed into my favorite pair of pajamas and then lay across the sofa with my tablet, wholly prepared to binge that new Netflix show everyone had been gushing about. Unfortunately, the opening credits hadn't even finished rolling before Merlin jumped up onto my chest and blocked my view of the portable screen.

"I've asked Luna to move in with us, and she's agreed," he informed me with a rumbling purr.

Well, this kind of felt like a thing he should have asked me first, but even I understood that Luna had nowhere else to go. And even though I'd never known great love myself, I clearly recognized it in these two. I wanted them to be together and happy, even if that meant adding another roommate.

"Congratulations," I said with a sleepy smile.

Merlin nodded at me. "Okay. Just making sure you knew how things would be. As you were."

While I tucked into my show, Merlin gave Luna the grand tour of our house, which wasn't all that grand, given its small size and outdated furniture. Still, I occasionally heard her gushing and exclaiming over things like the shower curtain, coffee maker, and litter box. True, the coffee maker was impressive, but the other things? I guess she preferred my grandma's hodgepodge aesthetic to Virginia's all florals all the time.

Somewhere into my third episode, the pet door opened and closed with a swish. I assumed the two lovebirds had gone out for a walk through the neighborhood, but a moment later, Luna jumped onto the coffee table and waited for me to pause my show before speaking.

"I sent Merlin out for a while," she said, adjusting herself into a more comfortable position. "To give us two girls some time to talk."

I sat up and patted the couch beside me. "What's up?"

Luna hopped over and took a quick breath before launching into what seemed to be a prepared speech. "At first I wasn't sure you were worthy of my Merlin. That's why I gave you such a hard time. But today you proved yourself more than worthy. You were very brave, but moreover, you were there for him in a terrifying situation. And you did not run or abandon him. I was wrong about you, and I want to apologize for that."

I blinked slowly as I took in the weight of her words. "Of course I was there for him, he's my cat. And now that you'll be living with us, I'll be there for you, too."

Luna began to purr. "It will be nice to have a human who loves me for a change. Virginia only loved my power. I should have taken more care in choosing, but I was hurt and distracted, knowing that Merlin and I would have to end our relationship so we could each take our full places in the magical community." She paused for a moment. "I know we have only just met and that most of our encounters have been negative until now, but Merlin trusts you and that's good enough for me. I love you, as he loves you."

"Thank you, Luna," I whispered softly. "That means a lot."

She rubbed her nose against my face in affection, but I pulled back and let out a pained hiss.

"What's the matter?" Luna asked, concern reflecting in her cornflower eyes.

"Dash gave me a nasty cut," I said, raising my fingers to my face and wincing again.

"Oh, no," she wailed. "Merlin and I were so caught up in each other that we didn't tend to your wounds. The moment he is returned, he'll whip you up a nice salve."

"That would be nice," I admitted, unable to refuse the promise of help.

"Are you hurt anywhere else?" Luna wanted to know.

"My shoulders are sore from being handcuffed so long, but Dash didn't touch me at all. Except when she slashed me. It was really weird, actually. She looked at my blood and said it explained a few things. What do you think she meant by that?"

Luna shook her head. "I don't know. Normally illusion witches can't read biomatter, so if Dash did, she is exceptionally powerful."

I shuddered at this. "Well, that definitely doesn't make me any less afraid for our next battle."

"No." Luna stared off into the distance as if seeing something I couldn't. "But there is a way to learn what she knows."

"Oh?" Now she had my interest.

"Has Merlin told you about Nocturna?"

I shook my head, even though the movement caused the cut to sting all the more.

"It's only accessible at night, but many of our kind live in the open there," Luna explained in almost a whisper, as if the place itself were sacred. "We can take you, find a blood witch, have him tell us what he sees there."

"Can we go tonight?" I asked, hope creeping up anew.

"I don't see why not. It will be up to Merlin to decide, though. He's the only one of us with a magical passport now."

"Okay, I'll ask when he gets home, then," I said with a small smile of gratitude.

"Actually, sweetie. Leave that part to me. I know

exactly how to get a yes from our Merlin." She winked, then hopped away.

I cringed but thankfully avoided summoning a mental picture of what Luna's persuasive methods might entail. I already had enough to worry about, thank you very much.

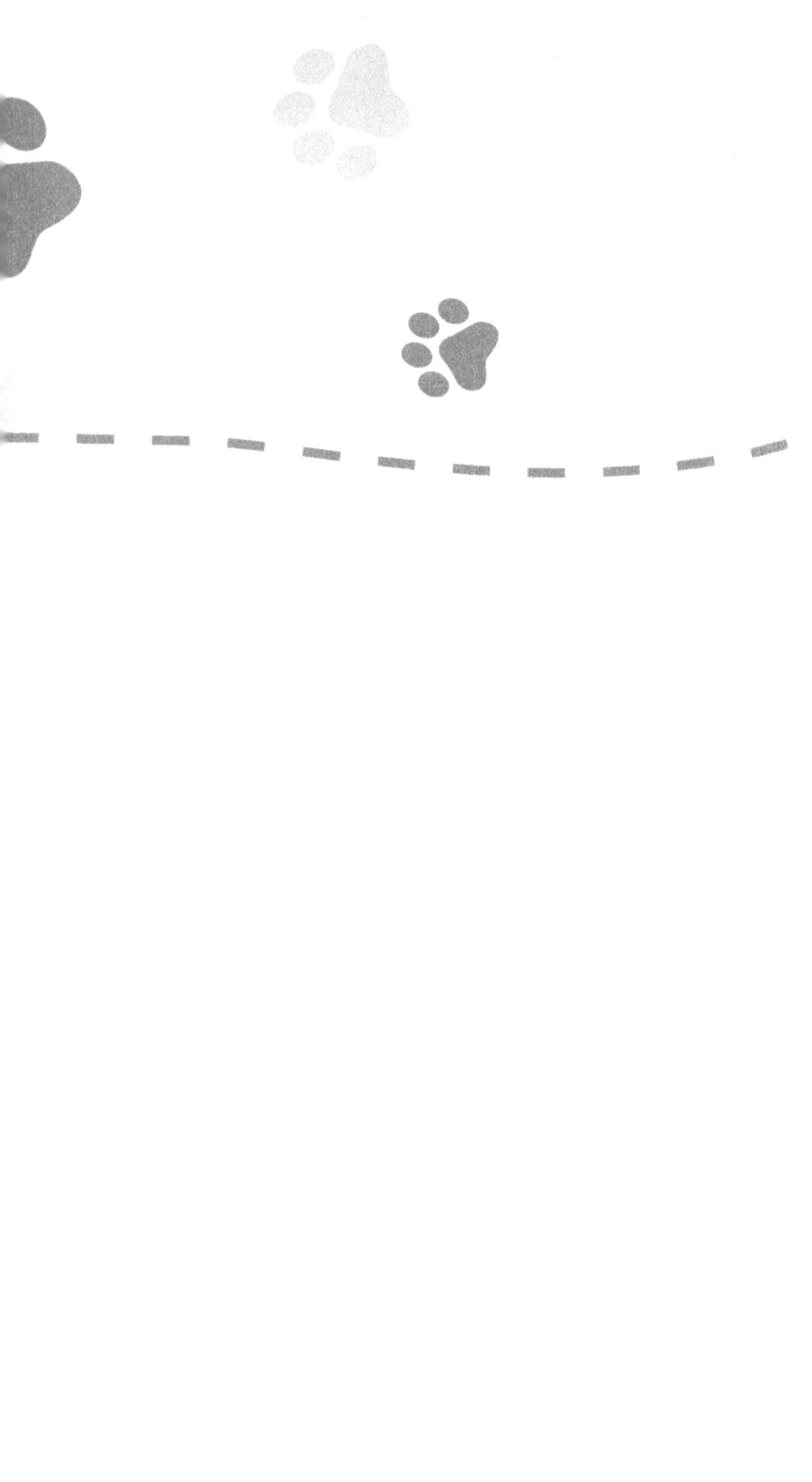

29

At this point I was just stalling. I knew I'd need to be up and active at night to visit the magical city Luna had called Nocturna, but before we could go, there was one more thing I needed to handle today.

After a quick conversation with Merlin to confirm I could actually do what I had planned, I shot Kelley a text asking her if we could meet up. She invited me to come out to the coffeehouse for another round of PSLs and frozen banana nut bread.

By the time I had fetched my car and driven over to Harold's, I found her working with the espresso machine. A big smile stretched across her face when she spotted me.

I raced over to hug her. "You look so much better today. Does this mean you got good news?"

Kelley's smile widened. "My dad's lawyer contacted me today about the will. He changed it up about four weeks ago and left it all to me. He may not have taken much opportunity to get to know me, Gracie, but my father did love me."

I hugged her again. "Oh, I always knew he did!" I cooed, even though I'd honestly had no idea. "He probably just wanted to be careful about how he approached your relationship, figuring he had more time."

We both became somber.

"I'm sure you're right," Kelley said.

"Officer Dash contacted me today," I revealed. This would be the only part of my confession that was actually true, but I knew Kelley would need to hear this in order to move on. "Your dad wasn't murdered, after all. He had a heart attack. The medical examiner who suggested he'd died by poison was fired for getting it so wrong."

"I'm glad he wasn't murdered," Kelley said, "But I'm still so sad that he's gone."

She finished preparing our lattes and we relocated to the big corner booth. Of course, I still hadn't revealed the biggest part of my plan but knew I couldn't put it off much longer or I'd risk losing the nerve.

"So what's next for you, Kelley? Will you be going back to Ohio with your mom?"

She shook her head. "No, definitely not. I mean, why would I do that when I now have my own business to run?"

"You mean...?"

"Yes! The coffee shop is mine. I'm going to be making some big changes to the menu and to the payroll... you should definitely be making more than you currently are... but I'm going to keep the name in honor of Dad."

"That's wonderful, Kelley. You'll be a great boss, and I can't wait to hear all your ideas!"

As it turned out, she couldn't wait to share them with me. "I can go over some of them now if you'd like. To start, PSL is no longer a seasonal item. We'll serve it all year round. And also—"

"I hate to interrupt, especially because I love that idea so much, but there's something I need to say," I said, my heart thumping hard in my chest.

Kelley looked at me with concern.

"Nothing's wrong," I promised.

"Then what's going on?" she pressed.

I reached into my purse and took out an empty

water bottle. Merlin had helped me prepare the potion I requested, even though he warned me against it more than once. Still, I knew I was making the right decision with this.

I uncapped the water bottle and set it in the middle of the table. Nothing happened. At least that's how it looked to those who didn't know it held an invisible form of magic.

"What's with the empty bottle?" Kelley asked with one eyebrow raised.

"Don't worry about that," I said, waiting for her to shift her gaze back to me.

I didn't continue until her eyes met mine. "This is kind of a weird question, but I want you to tell me the first answer that pops into your head. Okay?"

Kelley shrugged, but said, "Okay."

"If you could wish for anything, anything in the whole wide world, what would you ask for?"

She snorted. "Like a fairy godmother kind of thing?"

"Something like that," I answered with a secretive smile. "You don't have to blurt it out. You can take a moment if you need to, but not much longer. So, tell me, what's your one big wish?"

A smile blossomed from cheek to cheek. "Well, I guess I—"

"Wait," I cried, reaching over to the bottle and giving it a good squeeze. "Take a deep breath first," I instructed, wanting to be sure she breathed it all in.

I watched as Kelley sucked in the invisible gaseous potion, waiting nervously to hear what she would say next.

But she knew exactly what she wanted. "I want to honor my dad's legacy by making Harold's House of Coffee the most successful coffee shop this town has ever seen," she said with a firm-set jaw.

"You will," I promised her.

After all, I'd just passed on my ask-for-anything familiar spell. Merlin had told me I shouldn't, because he wouldn't be able to make another one. And, yeah, now I could never get to be Lady Gaga, or King Arthur, or someone else crazy famous...

But Kelley needed this more than I did, and giving her this once-in-a-lifetime opportunity felt right, considering all she'd lost because of us.

I couldn't bring Harold back, but I could make sure his daughter was well taken care of in his absence, and that's exactly what I planned to do.

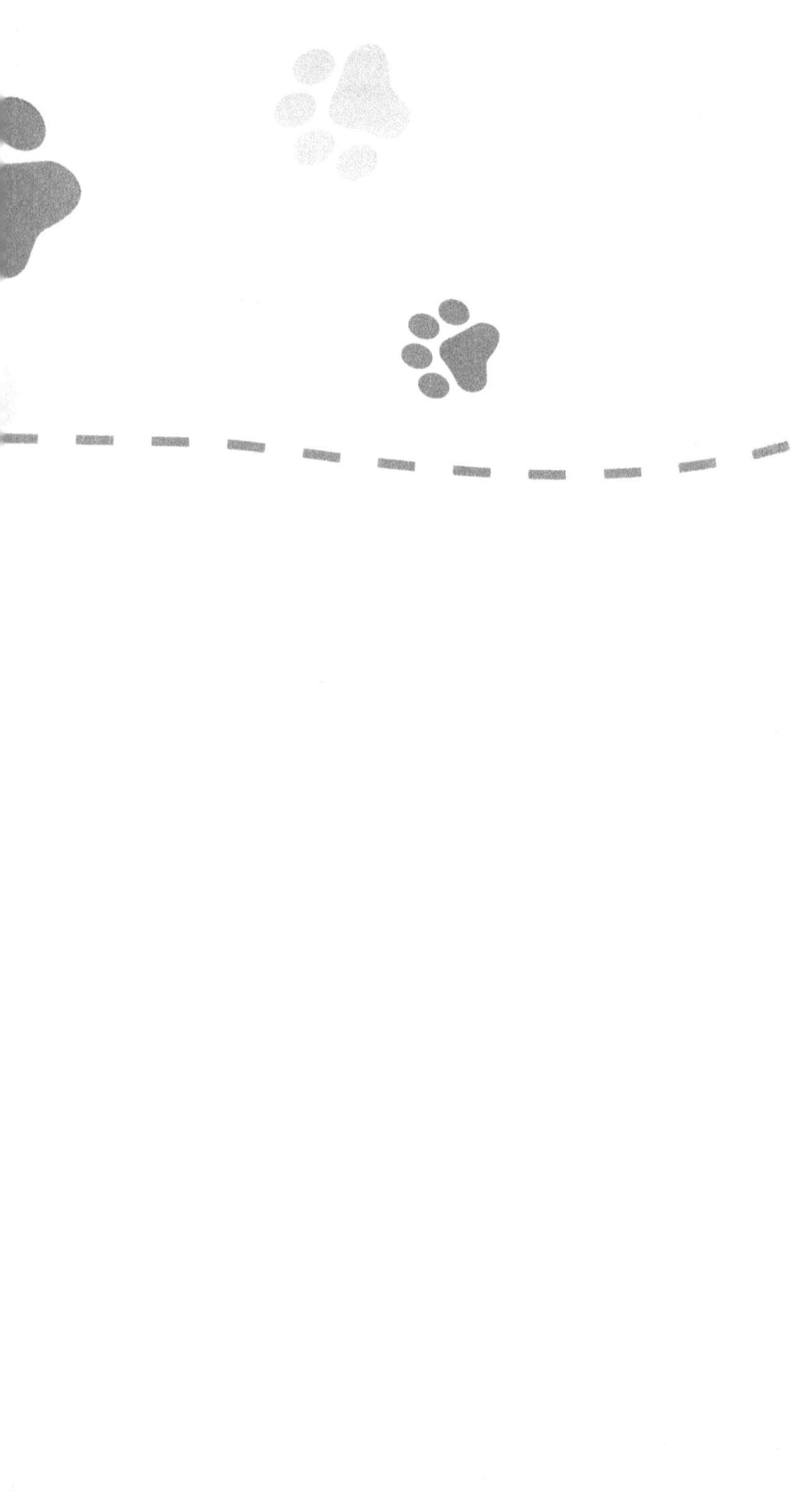

30

When I came home, I showed both cats the empty bottle I'd used to pass my wish on to Kelley.

"Yup, it's gone," Merlin whined, rolling onto his side dramatically. "I can't believe you gave that away."

"She's a good one," Luna told Merlin as she pressed her body against the side of my leg and shook her sleek white tail. "My familiar destroyed herself by craving power. Yours freely gave it away. You're a lucky witch."

"That, I am," Merlin admitted with a wink. "Even if she is a little bit crazy."

"What's done is done," I said with a shrug. Before I'd gone to see Kelley, Merlin had whipped up an antipain potion, taking the hurt out of both my shoulders and my cheek, which meant I could move freely now. "Let's focus on what we can still hope to change."

"Are you sure you're ready to enter Nocturna?" Merlin asked me tersely. "It's rather overwhelming for a first-timer, especially one so new to magic as you are."

"I'm sure," I said, pressing my lips into a tight line. "I'd rather have the knowledge than not."

"The sun is setting," Luna said, and we both stared at Merlin, waiting for him to speak.

"Then let's go," he acquiesced.

I followed Merlin as he slowly stalked toward the door.

He ran through, but Luna waited for me to open the big door. "Remember, you can do this," she assured me with a simple smile.

I took in a deep breath and stepped outside into the evening twilight.

Merlin had already seated himself upon the bird bath. "The moment the sun disappears over the horizon, we'll be able to use the cauldron as a doorway to Nocturna. Shouldn't be long now."

"How am I going to fit through that?" I squeaked, studying the small stone fountain.

"Magic, duh!" Luna answered with a laugh and then hopped up beside Merlin.

"Step forward," he said as he splashed in the water and placed a wet paw on Luna's forehead.

"Lean in close," he instructed. When I did, he dipped his paw again and touched it to my head. "Luna will go through first, and I'll go in last to make sure nothing goes awry."

"Goes awry? Wait. Does that mean this is dangerous?"

"Don't worry about it, sweetie," Luna cooed.

In the distance the sun finished its descent. The cauldron glowed a bright mint green, swallowing Luna whole.

"Whoa, I don't want to do this!" I whined and took a giant leap back.

"Too late," Merlin said, then summoned a gust of wind that sent me stumbling right into the fountain. I closed my eyes as I braced for impact, and I screamed and screamed and screamed, until I noticed that everything was absolutely fine.

When I opened my eyes again, I stood on a dark stone path. Both cats were at my side. The surrounding buildings had been built in a Bavarian style, white with dark crossbeams.

Luna nudged me forward. "What do you think?"

"It looks like something out of a fairytale," I said, instantly falling in love with the quaint magical city.

"This area was settled during peak popularity of the Brothers Grimm. Everyone wanted the German village look, and Nocturna was no different," she explained with obvious pride.

"Where is everybody?" I asked.

"Just waking up, no doubt. Remember, we cats tend to keep evening hours," Luna reminded me, and of course she was right.

"Follow me," Merlin commanded, and Luna and I both fell into step beside him. He led us to what appeared to be a covered wagon, although it had nothing hooked up to pull it.

"We need a reading," Merlin shouted from outside.

A moment later, a flame point Siamese popped its head out from the wagon. Its eyes grew wide as it caught sight of Merlin. "And what will you be offering in trade?"

"Anything but lightning," Merlin responded, standing tall as he waited.

"How about a rainstorm?" the Siamese asked greedily.

"Done," Merlin answered with a nod.

"Excellent. Now let's see what we have here."

Luna guided me toward the wagon. "Go on, sit down."

"But doesn't Merlin have to pay first?" I whispered to her.

"They have a spoken contract bound by magic," she explained. "Don't worry, everything will be taken care of."

"Is this going to hurt?" I asked the flame point who'd popped up beside me on the bench seat.

He scoffed. "I'm insulted. What kind of blood witch do you take me for?"

I fell silent, preferring not to discuss how badly Dash had hurt me when she took my blood. The Siamese blood witch moved to my lap, then held his paw to my neck. I felt nothing, but when he pulled away, blood tipped each of his claws, shimmering in the night sky.

He stared down at his paw with wide eyes. "Well, I'll be."

"What? What is it?" Merlin demanded, sounding even more nervous than I felt.

"This is your familiar?" the blood witch asked, glancing from his paw to me and then back again.

"Yes, she is. Is everything okay?"

"More than okay!" the Siamese crooned, as if hysterically happy. "Her blood is especially powerful. She's a descendant of the original dutiful familiar."

"Arthur?" Luna asked with a gasp.

"King Arthur, the Great Merlin's true companion," the Siamese verified.

"And you're descended from Merlin?" I asked him, recalling the story he'd told me when we first spoke.

My cat nodded but continued to stare blankly ahead.

"What does this mean?" I asked weakly, still unsure of how to take the news.

"It means that you have the most powerful bond of any witch and familiar living today," Luna supplied in a hushed whisper.

"No wonder we bonded so fast," Merlin murmured.

"We already knew about the bond," I pointed out.

"Yes," the Siamese said. "But keep it a carefully

guarded secret, for there will be many who wish to separate you."

I nodded dumbly, terrified of what I'd just learned.

Dash already knew…

And she'd definitely be back.

You already know that Gracie and Merlin's magical adventures are far from over. Ready to find out what happens next?

Get your copy of *Merlin Fights a Ghost* so that you can keep reading this series today!

Pssst… If you absolutely loved this book and want even more, make sure you **sign up for Molly's newsletter**. When you do, you'll receive an exclusive digital prize pack, including a free book!

WHAT'S NEXT?

It was hard enough serving as my witchy cat's familiar when we only had to deal with threats we could see. Now he's gotten himself into a bitter feud with a newly dispatched ghost, leaving me to wonder... How in the heck are we supposed to defeat this thing?

I miss the simple days when all I had to worry about was finishing my thesis paper and not getting fired from my part-time job as a barista.

And, yeah, even though I didn't choose the magic life, it sure as heck chose me. Now all I have to do is to keep myself alive long enough to appreciate some of the perks.

MERLIN FIGHTS A GHOST is now available.

Get your copy so that you can keep reading this series today!

Hello, I'm Gracie Springs. I used to be a pretty normal girl, until about a week ago. You see, my boss got murdered by magic, and an evil witch and her accomplice tried to frame me for it.

As it turns out, I'm descended from King Arthur. I've also been chosen to serve as my witchy cat's familiar. I used to call him Fluffy, but now I know he much prefers to go by Merlin. He has a famous lineage, too. He's descended from the original Merlin.

No, not the human imposter everyone thinks they know. The real wizard, who just so happened to be a cat.

Because of our intertwined ancestry, Merlin and I have an almost unbreakable bond. *Almost.*

The bad guy got away last time, but we both know she'll be back with a new plan to steal Merlin's magic from him for good.

While all this is going on, I also have to keep up the appearances of a normal life by working my part-time job as a barista at Harold's House of Coffee. The shop is in the process of being remodeled, thanks to the very ambitious goals of Harold's predecessor, his long-lost daughter, Kelley.

Also, I am very close to completing my master's degree in Sociology. I just have to finish my thesis, and then I can find work in my field rather than forever working as a part-time bean-slinger.

Lately, I'm plenty busy with getting the hang of my new role as a familiar. Both Merlin and his new girlfriend are more than happy to grill me at all hours of the day and night.

I need to be ready for when the next attack happens, and make no mistake, we all know it's coming soon.

I bet my grandma never would have guessed what was in store for me when she gifted me her small-town Georgia home and retired to the Florida Keys. She certainly didn't know that a certain magical Maine Coon had already been scoping her out to work as her familiar, or that he'd later choose me in her place.

Honestly, even though my life has taken a turn for the crazy, I wouldn't have it any other way. I love Merlin, and I love our adventures together, no matter how much they frighten the frijoles out of me.

I can't cast magic, but that doesn't mean I'm not important in the fight against the wicked illusion witch who has set our sights on us.

This time when she finds us again, I'll be ready to take her down.

* * *

An unholy shriek woke me from a dead sleep.

Meeeeeeeeeeh!

I darted upright in bed and grabbed my cell phone to serve as a flashlight. "Who's there?" I demanded.

But was only answered by Merlin, thumping down the hardwood floor in the hallway.

Meeeeeeeeeh! the shriek sounded again, and this time I realized it was Luna crying her heart out.

And so it went. Shriek, scamper. Shriek, scamper. Until at last I made my way into the hall and found them both staring at the far corner of the ceiling with their ears pressed back against their little kitty heads.

"What's going on?" I asked, knowing full well both of them were capable of more than just uncivilized meows.

"Gh-gh-gh-ghost," Merlin said, then took another sprint down the short hallway.

I glanced up to the spot where Luna still had her large unblinking eyes fixed... and saw absolutely nothing.

"What do you see?" I asked her. Generally, she was the more logical of the two—or at least the one more likely to open up to me.

"I can't see anything," she whispered without removing her gaze from the ceiling. "But there's an energy that's forming. It's not wholly in our world yet, but it will be soon."

"So you see a pre-ghost?" I summarized.

"Something like that."

"But how can you tell? You're not magical anymore," I reminded her.

Luna couldn't stifle the hiss that escaped her. "I may not be a witch, but I am still a cat. Magical or not, we can all see into the supernatural realm."

"Like Nocturna?" I asked, referring to the magical nighttime city that was only accessible to magical creatures at the twilight hour.

Merlin growled and began to kick up his hind legs.

"Oh, no, you don't!" I cried, reaching down to pluck him into my arms. "No tornadoes inside the house."

He growled in dismay until I set him back down.

"We must get rid of it before it takes its full form," Luna told me as she worried her bottom lip with her top fangs.

"The fact that it's here so soon in its after-life journey is a very bad sign," Merlin revealed, and when I looked down at him he had arched his back and puffed up to maximum volume.

I grabbed him into my arms again. "Definitely no lightning inside the house!"

"Then what should we do?" Luna asked with a gasp.

"Let me make some coffee," I said, admitting defeat at last. It was clear that neither cat would let me go to bed until I found a way to bust this newborn ghost... or at least to send it off to haunt some place far, far away from here.

MERLIN FIGHTS A GHOST is now available.

Get your copy so that you can keep reading this series today!

ABOUT MOLLY FITZ

While *USA Today bestselling* author Molly Fitz can't technically talk to animals, she and her three feline writing assistants have deep and very animated conversations as they navigate their days.

She lives with her child and their own private zoo somewhere in the wilds of Alaska. Molly will occasionally venture out for good food, great coffee, or to meet new animal friends.

Learn more about Molly and her books, and be sure to sign up for her newsletter at **www.Molly Mysteries.com**.

ALSO BY MOLLY FITZ

Learn more about Molly's collected works, so that you can decide which book you'd like to read next...

PET WHISPERER P.I.

Angie Russo just partnered up with Blueberry Bay's first ever talking cat detective. Along with his ragtag gang of human and animal helpers, Octo-Cat is determined to save the day... so long as it doesn't interfere with his schedule.

Start with book 1, ***Kitty Confidential***.

MERLIN'S MAGICAL MYSTERIES

Gracie Springs is not a witch... but her cat is. Now she must help to keep his secret or risk spending the rest of her life in some magical prison. Too bad trouble seems to find them at every turn!

Start with book 1, ***Merlin Takes a Familiar***.

PARANORMAL TEMP AGENCY

Tawny Bigford's simple life takes a turn for the magical when she stumbles upon her landlady's murder and is recruited by a talking black cat named Fluffikins to take over the deceased's role as the official Town Witch for Beech Grove, Georgia.

Start with book 1, ***Witch for Hire***.

THE MYSTERIES OF MOONLIGHT MANOR (WITH TRIXIE SILVERTALE)

Sydney Coleman has it all—until she doesn't. No sooner does she launch her bed and breakfast, than a trio of ghosts turn up oppose her at every turn. They insist she solve the murder of their mistress, but Sydney is desperate for cash. If she can't book some guests fast, her haunted mansion is utterly doomed.

Start with book 1, ***Moonlight & Mischief.***

CONNECT WITH MOLLY

Sign up for my newsletter and get a special digital prize pack for joining, including an exclusive story, *Meowy Christmas Mayhem*, fun quiz, and lots of cat pictures!

Sign up: **MollyMysteries.com/subscribe**

Now, if you ever wished you could converse with cats, here's your opportunity! This is me officially inviting you into my whacky inner world as part of my Cozy Kitty Book Club.

For those who just can't get enough of my zany cat characters and their hapless humans, this book club will provide new content to devour and the chance to get to know my best author friends.

From exclusive stories, behind-the-scenes trivia to never-before-released bonus content, and monthly giveaways, there's a lot to love about the Cozy Kitty Book Club. Join today to find out what we're reading next!

Join: **MollyMysteries.com/club**